DIE FREE,
DIE HARD!

The Indian yells were loud in Jake's ears. He heard shots again, and something kicked up dirt nearby. He pulled his horse to the ground and onto its side. He wanted to shoot the animal, but each bullet was precious now. In the few seconds remaining to him, he took cover behind the dying horse. He drew his Sharps rifle and a handful of cartridges and laid them on the saddle. He laid his revolvers there, too, with the spare cylinders from the saddlebags. He intended to sell his life as dearly as possible. He would save one bullet for himself, though. He would kill himself rather than become a prisoner. . . .

Fawcett Gold Medal Books
by Robert W. Broomall:

THE BANK ROBBER

DEAD MAN'S CANYON

DEAD MAN'S CROSSING

DEAD MAN'S CROSSING

Robert W. Broomall

FAWCETT GOLD MEDAL • NEW YORK

A Fawcett Gold Medal Book
Published by Ballantine Books
Copyright © 1987 by Robert W. Broomall

Library of Congress Catalog Card Number: 86-91820

ISBN 0-449-13116-5

Printed in Canada

First Edition: May 1987

1

On a rainy spring morning in 1854, the population of San Antonio converged on the Main Plaza. They were going to a hanging.

Jake Moran stood beneath the awning of the Black Cat Saloon. He wiped beer from his drooping mustache with the back of his hand. He hated hangings. He had seen too many hangings, too much frontier justice. There was no sense staying around the saloon, though. He'd only gone in there for the free bar food, and after he'd spent his last two bits on beer, they had thrown him out.

Jake pulled down his wide-brimmed black hat. He turned up his collar. He hunched his shoulders and stepped into crowded Market Street, which was churned into a muddy porridge after two days of rain. Jake was twenty-six. He was tall and lean and roughly handsome, with angular features, reddish-brown hair, and fearsome burn scars on his hands. He wore high boots, a patched coat, and a faded red flannel shirt with a long bandana. He carried two .36 Navy Colt revolvers—one on his left hip, one behind his back.

The flow of the crowd carried Jake toward the plaza. Clomping through the ankle-deep mud beside him were Americans and Mexicans and blacks. There were men and women, plainsmen and farmers, vaqueros and soldiers and clerks. There were idlers and hardcases of every description. Wagons and animals and solid-wheeled Mexican *carettas* added to the confusion. Children darted everywhere.

The Texas sky was a lumpy gray. The northwest wind gusted with rain. Across the river, where the emigrant camps lay, long black columns of smoke rose against the gloom. They were burning the dead over there, burning their possessions as well. The wind blew the smoke away from the city, but it could not keep the sickening cholera stench out of the air.

The emigrants had brought the cholera here from Brazos Santiago, at the mouth of the Rio Grande. In the camps, the emigrants were dying by the dozen. Soon the disease would sweep the city; already rumor said there were cases among the Mexicans. Jake had nearly died from malaria in Panama; he had no wish to try cholera. Those who could were leaving San Antonio, fast. Jake had to get out, too— but how, without money or a horse?

Someone tapped his shoulder, and a voice said, "Say, friend, aren't you Jake Moran? Lieutenant Moran of the Tennessee Volunteers?"

Jake turned. He found himself facing a wiry, strong-looking man, with shoulder-length hair and a long gray beard. The man wore a floppy hat, his greasy buckskins were decorated with beads and fringes, and even in the rain he smelled of buffalo. He carried a Sharps rifle in a fringed scabbard, and he wore a brace of Colt revolvers in hand-made buckskin holsters.

"I'm Moran," Jake said, "but I'm a captain now, in the California Militia."

"I knew it." The man's accent was surprisingly genteel for his dress. "I wouldn't forget you, not even with that mustache. I saw you at Chapultapec. Not your face, of course, but you were pointed out to me later, at the victory parade. You were a corporal then. After they made you an officer, you were a guest of my regimental mess—the Mississippi Fusiliers."

"Oh, yes." Jake had a boozy recollection of ragged, filthy, wild-haired officers eating mule meat off silver, served by liveried slaves. Jake had been a guest of many regimental messes after Chapultepec.

The frontiersman turned to his two companions. The first was a delicate, flaxen-haired man, who squinted nearsightedly in the rain. He was dressed much like Jake, except his clothes were new and he wore his revolvers awkwardly, as if he were unused to them. The second man was handsome and well groomed, smoking a cheroot with a languid air. He wore an expensive shooting jacket and a wide-brimmed straw hat. Behind him stood a tall, well-built black man, probably his body slave.

"Captain Moran was the first man into Chapultepec," the frontiersman explained. "I watched the attack from General Scott's position on Tucubaya. Our first line had been shot to pieces by artillery and rifle fire. Our second line was being pounded. The men were ready to break. The battle hung in the balance. Then one man—Captain Moran, here—rose from the wreckage. He staggered forward alone, toward a small breach in the wall, determined to conquer or die. The rest of our boys saw his example, and I tell you they gave a cheer that made your hair stand on end. Then they raised their scaling ladders and went charging after him."

The frontiersman went on admiringly, "That was the bravest deed I've ever seen, and, believe me, I've seen a few. It chills me yet. How many bayonet wounds did you take that day, Captain—ten?"

"Nine," mumbled Jake. He looked down, a gesture that some might have taken for modesty. He did not tell the frontiersman—as he had never told anyone—that he had been dazed with shock and terror that day at Chapultepec. He didn't tell how he had been trying to surrender when he had stumbled into that breach and had accidentally become a hero.

The frontiersman extended a hand, "I'm Israel Combs."

Jake started to take the hand, then stopped. "*The* Israel Combs?"

"That's me."

Jake found himself staring stupidly. He'd expected Israel Combs to be taller, a giant, befitting his exploits. Unlike Jake, Israel Combs was a real hero. A lawyer by training, he had fought at San Jacinto. He'd been on the Mier Expedition in Mexico, where the captives drew beans to determine who was to be executed. He'd been a Texas Ranger, a major of Mississippi infantry, and God knew what else during his famous career. Not for the first time, Jake was plunged into a black hatred of himself, a hatred of his own life of deceit and fraud, all built upon that one moment in the breach at Chapultepec. He'd made such a point about being a captain, too. As if he deserved it.

Combs introduced his companions, who seemed impressed, making Jake feel even worse. The nearsighted man was a newspaper editor named Webb—"Captain Moran, this is a great honor." The dandy with the slave was Langdon Molyneaux—"A pleasure, sir. A genuine pleasure."

They moved on, forced to by the crowd. They entered the plaza. A scaffold stood in the plaza's center, its hempen noose dangling in the rain. To one side of the scaffold, in front of the old limestone Council House, a brass band pumped away enthusiastically, if not on key. Vendors made their way through the press, selling whiskey and beer, tamales and frijoles and tortillas. The air smelled of wet wool and cigar smoke.

Even here, in the relative safety of San Antonio, Combs's pale blue eyes never stopped moving, never stopped watching. "What brings you to Texas, Captain?"' he asked.

"Call me Jake. I been scouting for the Army. We was surveying possible railroad routes to California. We wintered at Coons Ranch, across the Rio Grande from El Paso del Norte. We pulled in here two weeks ago. I had a job lined up with a freight outfit, but the company went bust. Now I'm looking to get out before the cholera hits."

Around them, the crowd began cheering. The brass band broke into "Old Hundred." The condemned man was being led out. The onlookers jostled for a better view, and fights broke out as men struggled to keep out of the puddles that dotted the plaza. Through the craning necks and heads, Jake glimpsed the prisoner, a young Mexican, heavily guarded lest his friends try to rescue him.

"Did you discover a route?" Combs shouted above the commotion.

"Yes," Jake said.

"Is it passable for wagons? Without improvements?"

"It is."

Combs's eyes narrowed. He looked at Jake keenly. "Where are you headed now?"

Jake shrugged. "New Orleans. Then back to San Francisco by ship. That's the plan, anyway."

"Well, *there's* a coincidence. We're headed for San Francisco, too—all except Molyneaux, here. He's leaving us in Tucson. Can't bring slaves into California, you know."

Molyneaux gestured expansively with the cheroot, as if he were used to being master of all he surveyed. "Our land in Georgia is about played out. My family sent me to investigate the Santa Cruz Valley, to see if it's suitable for cotton. We originally planned to move to Texas, but there's too damn many German immigrants and Mexicans here 'bouts. They get too familiar with the niggers. It makes the niggers forget their place." Behind him, his slave stood impassively, as if he didn't hear.

Combs went on, "We planned on taking the Lower Road into Mexico, then up through Arizona to the Gila Valley; but if you say there's a route all the way through U.S. territory . . ." He leaned in closer. "Look, why don't you come with us, Jake? Show us this new trail. You can be my assistant hunter and scout. I'm not authorized to pay you money—I wish I was—but your wages will be use of our horse herd and supplies. I'll make good any equipment you lack. You won't get rich, but you'll get to California a damn sight faster'n you would by ship. What do you say? We pull out at first light tomorrow. 'Hampton's California Company' we call ourselves. The promoter is Tyler Hampton. He's supposed to be here, but I can't find him in this mob.''

Shielding himself from the rain, Jake rolled a *cigarito* and considered Combs's offer. The California Company faced fifteen hundred miles of Comanches and Apaches and Yumas. They faced the hellish wastes of Arizona and the Mojave. Jake had just made that journey with a troop of the Second Dragoons, the Army's crack regiment. It was a journey he never wanted to make again, especially with a bunch of raw emigrants.

The cheering grew louder now as the condemned man mounted the scaffold. The Americans were cheering the young man's imminent death; the Mexicans were encouraging him to be brave. The flat-faced young man was dressed in filthy white cotton, plastered to his body by the rain. He put up a front for his supporters, grinning and waving his bound hands.

Jake put the *cigarito* in his mouth and lit it, cupping his scarred hands, squinting against the slanting raindrops. "How big a train you got?"

"Ten wagons, twenty-three men, three women, and two kids," Combs said. "Supplies are ample. The horses and cattle are fair, considering what we had to pick from."

"A small party," Jake observed.

"Hampton says there's a lot more coming in, but there's no time to wait for 'em—not if we're to beat the cholera."

"What about the Indians?"

Combs's eyes narrowed, and the skin around them crinkled like parchment. "We'll have to take our chances with the Indians. Are you with us?"

Jake dragged on the *cigarito*. He didn't want to go to California with these emigrants. It was too dangerous. Across the plaza, he saw a pretty Mexican girl with a flower in her hair. She and her friends were shouting encouragement to the condemned man. Behind her, the dark columns of smoke rose higher. By this time next week, that girl might be dead of cholera. So might Jake, if he stayed.

He dropped the half-smoked *cigarito* into the mud. "I'm with you."

The frontiersman grinned through his sodden beard. "Good, good. We can use you. I can promise you some excellent hunting, if nothing else."

Webb and Molyneaux were enthusiastic. "Glad to have you with us, Captain," the newspaperman said.

"Look forward to your company," Molyneaux said. "Do you play p—?"

He stopped. A man was watching them. A big, dark-visaged man in a blue coat. The big man moved closer, head and shoulders thrust forward, pushing aside Molyneaux's slave, who stood in his way. The slave's eyes narrowed with anger, but he said nothing. The big man looked at Jake with arrogant, cruel eyes, then turned to Combs. "You work for me, Combs. Don't forget that. I decide who comes with us, not you."

Combs stood straighter. "And the company elected me captain, Hampton. Don't you forget that. I do the hiring and firing on this expedition. A man like Captain Moran will be invaluable if we run into trouble. Besides, he knows a new—"

"I have enough men on my payroll now," Hampton said. "I don't need another."

"Well, I want him, and I'm not used to having my judgment questioned. Captain Moran comes with us or I'm leaving. Find yourself another guide to California—if you can."

Hampton flushed with rage, and for a second Jake thought he would strike the frontiersman. Combs didn't flinch, though, and Hampton's wrath grew as he realized that Combs was right—it was too late to hire another guide, especially one with the reputation of Israel Combs.

Hampton began breathing heavily, like a penned bull.

From beneath his thick brows, he looked at Jake with dislike. "Very well. He can come."

Combs smiled wryly. "Thank you. Jake, if you haven't guessed, this is the Honorable Tyler Hampton, late of the South Carolina Assembly. Hampton, meet Jake Moran, of Tennessee and California."

Jake held out his hand. Hampton did not take it.

Jake forced himself to meet the big man's glare coolly. He withdrew his hand with a smile, as if he didn't give a damn whether Hampton shook with him or not.

Hampton's thick lip curled. He was about to say something when the noisy crowd grew even more active. On the scaffold, a deputy was strapping weights to the condemned man's feet. The brass band stopped playing, and the sheriff stepped forward to read the charge, shouting to be heard above the crowd and the rain. The young Mexican had been convicted of stealing a horse. Probably the Mexican could not understand a word of the charge against him. Probably his only crime was being a Mexican.

A black-robed priest prayed for the condemned man's soul while the sheriff started to place a leather hood over his head. Suddenly the young Mexican spat in the sheriff's face. He struggled away and cursed the sheriff in Spanish. The Americans in the crowd howled with anger, while the Mexicans egged their man on. The guards backed closer to the scaffold, rifles raised, afraid of a riot. The sheriff grabbed the Mexican by the shirt and slapped him hard, drawing blood. The young man continued to resist, but the sheriff and the deputy jammed the noose over his head and adjusted it behind his left ear. Near Jake, one of San Antonio's many German citizens hoisted his son to his shoulders, saying, "Vatch now, Villy. Zis is vot happens to you ven you are not goot."

The angry sheriff wiped spit from his face. He placed his big hands on the trapdoor release. The Mexican was still struggling, still cursing. Beside Jake, the delicate-looking Webb watched the scene in horror. Molyneaux cast an appraising eye, as though judging form, while his slave stared blankly over his shoulder. Tyler Hampton looked up and grinned, baring his yellow teeth like fangs.

Jake turned away. He had wanted to leave the plaza before this happened. He heard the rusty creak of the lever. He heard the slam of the trapdoor, and a heavy object dropped with a *thud*. The crowd roared, then it fell strangely silent, save for the little boy Willy, who was wailing with fright.

Israel Combs paid no heed to the body kicking spasmodically overhead. Probably he'd seen such sights too often to be moved by them. "Let's go get dry and open a jug of cactus juice," he said. "We'll welcome Captain Moran to the company in style."

Webb had gone chalky white. He was only too glad to get out of the plaza. So was Jake. The languid Molyneaux was stirred by the prospect of a drink.

"Coming, Hampton?" Combs asked.

The big man glared at the group. "No," he said. He nodded curtly to them, then he cast a warning eye at Jake and swaggered off through the mud.

All around them the crowd was breaking up. Some walked away subdued, others were talking or laughing or counting up the morning's profits. Jake followed with Combs and his new companions. Molyneaux's slave limped on a stiff right leg. The broken bell of San Fernando Church clunked mournfully in the background.

The congestion leaving the plaza was twice as heavy as that coming in. As they inched along, Jake said to Combs, "Thanks for what you did. Risking your own job to get me a place with the company. That was—"

"Forget it," Combs said. "I had to show Hampton who was boss. I've been looking for an excuse. Let a man like that once crowd you—even a little—and there's no end to it." He looked over at Jake. "Watch out for Hampton. He killed a man in South Carolina. That's why he's going to California."

"What happened?"

"The other fella was a politician, like Hampton. There was bad blood between 'em, something to do with the fella's wife. Molyneaux told me this last night. Apparently the fella made fun of Hampton on the floor of the Assembly. Whatever he said must have been bad medicine, because Hampton took after him as soon as they recessed."

"How'd he kill him?"

"Beat in his head with one of those weighted canes. Because Hampton was so prominent, no warrant was issued, on the understanding that he would leave the state. He's traveling with men that he calls 'teamsters,' but what they really are is hired guns."

Jake felt cold in the pit of his stomach. "Thanks for the advice," he said.

Molyneaux and Webb had fallen behind in the press. Jake and Combs stopped to wait for them. "How did you get involved with Hampton, anyway?" Jake asked. "If all you wanted to do was beat the cholera, you could have gone back to living on the prairie."

"I got involved for money." There was bitterness in Combs's voice. "Living on the prairie never made me a cent. I came to Texas originally planning to take up some land. I planned on building an empire here. Instead, I spent all my time chasing Indians and Mexicans, mostly for free. I'm not getting any younger; I need a steady income. I'm looking to get to California, and Hampton offered me a way to get there. I heard my old Ranger *compadre*, Jack Hays, is sheriff in San Francisco. I'm hoping he can get me a job."

"I know Jack Hays," Jake said. "I was one of his deputies before I took the scouting job."

Combs looked at him, new respect in the pale eyes. "You going back with him?"

"I don't know." Jake didn't want to be a lawman again—lawmen had a way of dying young. Hays had dragooned him into the job because of his reputation. Still, he was broke, and he might not be able to find anything else.

"Well, if you do, I'd be proud to work with you," Combs said.

Jake mumbled thanks and looked away. He wondered if Combs would have asked him to join the company if he had been plain Jake Moran, and not Jake Moran, the Hero of Chapultapec. Would Combs have risked his job if he had known the kind of man Jake really was?

Molyneaux and Webb caught up, and the party made its way from the plaza. Jake was freezing; his shoulders and back were sopping wet with rain. Cold rain dripped from the brim of his hat, and it had soaked through his worn boots.

What had he gotten himself into?

He didn't like this, not a bit. Fifteen hundred miles of deserts and Indians and Tyler Hampton, too. For a minute he thought about backing out. He thought about disappearing into the crowd. Then he remembered the cholera hospitals he had seen, from Mexico to Panama to the gold camps in California. He remembered the agonized men dying in pools of their own vomit and excrement. He couldn't endure that. He'd have to trust Israel Combs to pull the company through. He didn't think anyone else could do it.

Jake pulled his coat closer around him and followed Combs down the muddy street. Behind them, the plaza emptied, until, at last, no one was left. Only the corpse of the Mexican remained, swinging in the rain and the prairie breeze.

2

Jake saw Israel Combs a half-mile off and dismounted. The frontiersman circled his hand twice in the air, then pointed down. He had found something that he wanted Jake to see. Jake set his horse at an easy lope. Maybe Combs had turned up water.

They had been on the trail for two and a half weeks. They had left behind the live oaks and cottonwoods, the rich bottomlands and the ground made boggy by spring rains. They had entered an arid country, with horizons broken only by distant mountains to the north and south. It would be like this for another two hundred miles, until they reached Ysleta on the Rio Grande, just outside El Paso.

Jake topped a sandy swell. Far to his right, a long plume of dust hung suspended in the still morning air. Beneath the dust's vanguard he made out two lines of wagons crawling across the vast landscape. Behind the wagons, back where the dust was thickest, were the horse and cattle herds.

Hampton's California Company was moving in good order. They were trail-broken now. They had not brought the cholera from San Antonio; instead, they were suffering from another affliction—thirst. If they didn't find water soon, they'd have to cut the ration again.

Combs was still dismounted as Jake rode up. The bearded frontiersman was holding his rifle. He was poised and alert in a way that Jake had never seen him, and Jake knew that he had found something other than water.

Combs said nothing. He didn't have to. Jake spotted the horse droppings immediately.

Jake dismounted and knelt, holding his animal's reins. The droppings didn't look more than a day old, and the horse that made them had not been grain fed. Jake saw the marks of unshod ponies in the sand. There were four or five riders in the party. They were moving northwest in single file, riding light.

Jake took a deep breath. He straightened and scanned the empty horizon. "Comanches?"

"Or Lipans." Combs's pale blue eyes were also searching the horizon. "Comanches most likely. Could be they're scouting for game. Could be they're making for one of those new reservations up on the Brazos."

"Or it could be they're coming back from a raid," Jake said.

Combs nodded.

"Reckon they're still around?"

"Maybe. If they are, they know we're here. They can't miss all that dust." Combs moved for his saddle. "Let's you and me ride to that outcrop of rock. We can see better from there."

They mounted. Their heads and eyes were moving all the time, searching the points of the compass. Jake loosened his Sharps rifle in its scabbard. He checked the loads in his Navy Colts, even though he knew they were good. Combs cradled his rifle in his arms.

They started for the outcrop, one of the few landmarks on the featureless plain. They took a circuitous route, following gullies and depressions in the earth, so that they wouldn't be sky-lighted. They'd been on the lookout for hostile Indians since they had left San Antonio, but all they'd seen so far had been Tonkawas and peaceful Penateka Comanches, looking to trade. This time might be different.

What if it's not a small party? Jake wondered. What if there's more? He damned the cholera for not allowing time to recruit more men. He damned himself for spending all his money in El Paso, and he damned that freight company for going bust. Then he damned himself again for ever joining this expedition.

They emerged onto open ground, about halfway to the rocks. There they halted. Combs sat still as death—watching, listening, smelling. At last he eased his horse forward. He made for a dry wash the course of which ran near the rocks. He studied the ground as he rode. They reached the lip of the wash. Combs eased his rifle on his arm and led them down.

The wash was wide. Its sides were choked with tall weeds, drooping in the heat. Combs and Jake moved slowly down the center. Jake's horse began tossing his head, and Jake steadied him. Combs's paint pricked his ears.

Jake was afraid. He wanted to turn back. They couldn't turn back, though. If there was trouble here, it was their job to flush it out.

Combs halted. So did Jake.

Something was lying in the sand ahead. A bundle of cloth.

They moved forward. While Jake watched the wash, Combs dismounted and examined the cloth. Combs let out his breath slowly. He hung his head. Then he straightened and handed the cloth bundle to Jake, whose horse shied at the smell.

It was a woman's dress, made of settlers' brown homespun. It was rank with sweat and crusted with large bloodstains.

Jake let the garment fall to the ground. The flesh of his hands seemed to be crawling.

Combs's eyes had the look of a man who has seen this sort of thing too many times. He seemed to age as Jake watched. "Some buck was wearing that dress," he said. "He was here not long ago, too."

Near the dress was another trail of unshod ponies, another small party headed northwest. Jake looked around, straining his senses. The sun beat down. Insects buzzed. The weeds smelled foul.

"Think they're with the first bunch?" Jake said.

"Maybe. Maybe not." Combs remounted. "Get back to the wagons, Jake. Tell 'em what we found. Tell 'em to be on the *qui vive*. Tell 'em to strengthen the guard on the stock, especially the horses."

"What about you?" Jake asked.

"I'm going to look round some more."

Jake wheeled his horse. He was glad to get out of this wash, glad to head back to the relative safety of the wagons. Behind him, he heard a dull *thunk*, and Combs said, "Damn."

Jake turned. A two-foot arrow was embedded in the frontiersman's thigh. At that moment, the weeds erupted with yelling Indians, with arrows and gunshots and smoke.

"Run for it!" Combs shouted.

The two white men dug in their heels, and their terrified horses took off. They thundered down the wash and left it at the first cut, making for open ground, heading for the wagons. They raced across the sandy plain. Behind them at least a dozen mounted Indians appeared, as if conjured out of the soil. The Indians' bodies were painted black and red. Comanches. They were yelling, carrying lances and bows and shields, quirting their shaggy ponies to catch up.

Jake and the wounded Combs rode side by side, holding their horses back a bit, saving them for the final spurt. Jake prayed that his animal would not misstep and fall. He prayed that he would get out of this alive.

The Indians drew closer, their horses' hooves drumming rhythmically. Jake busted a shot at them with his revolver. He had no hope of hitting anything, but maybe it would slow them down.

It didn't.

The white men followed the contours of the land, sticking to level ground. The Indians knew the country better;

Jake saw a half dozen ranging to the right. Some of the remaining Comanches had drawn close enough to fire their bows. An arrow stuck in Jake's saddle, and another grazed his horse's rump.

A range of low hills blocked the way ahead. Jake and Combs rode right. They shot through the first gap in the hills only to meet the half-dozen Comanches coming at them from the other direction.

"Ride through them!" Combs yelled.

Heads low to their horses' necks, the white men charged. The Indians were a blur of paint and lances and feathered shields. The sides came together too quickly to think what to do. Jake heard Combs's rifle boom. He fired his revolver, thought he hit a horse. As he recocked the revolver, a copper-colored face rushed up at him and he shot at it. Someone screamed. A lance passed close to his ribs. He fired at another Indian but didn't see the effect.

Then they were through, and the dust of the wagons was ahead of them. The Comanches wheeled and galloped after, joining the party still on the white men's heels.

Arrows whizzed by. Combs dropped his rifle and clutched his neck. There was an arrow in it. Combs's reins fell from his hand. He slumped forward in his saddle, grasping his horse's mane and fighting to stay on. His hat blew off.

Jake holstered his revolver. He eased his galloping horse closer to that of Combs. The whoops of the Comanches were loud in his ears. He leaned out and grabbed for Combs's trailing right rein. He missed it. He swore and leaned out again. This time his fingers closed around the flapping leather. He straightened and dug his heels in hard. There was no holding back now. It was all or nothing.

Across the level ground they raced, Jake leading Combs's horse, the Comanches right behind and gaining. Jake's horse was struck by another arrow. So was Combs's. Jake prayed that one of the animals would not go down.

He prayed that Combs would hang in the saddle till they reached safety.

He could see the canvas-topped wagons now. They were halted in line. Christ, why hadn't they circled?

He made for the gap between the lines of wagons. The Comanches drew closer, yelling wildly. The drumming of their horses' hooves was right on top of him.

He saw Dan Essex, the ex-Navy lieutenant, come running from the wagons, carrying a rifle. Behind him was Woodhouse, the Englishman, silk hat cocked over one eye. They were followed by the farmer, Cutter, and some others. Essex stopped and raised the rifle. There was a puff of smoke, the flat report of a shot. One of the Comanche horses stumbled, and its rider broke away from the charging mass. Woodhouse and the others opened fire as well. Jake heard a cry of pain, and the Comanches began drawing back. Then there was a gruff shout, and Tyler Hampton led a mounted charge from behind the wagons. The Comanches turned in retreat, screaming defiance, while Hampton and his party galloped past Jake, yelling their own war cries and firing revolvers.

Jake eased the horses off. He reined in midway down the line of wagons. Men came running up. He heard distant shots. Molyneaux's slave, Culpepper, took the horses. The newspaper editor, Webb, who was wearing glasses now, and some of the other men slid Combs from his saddle while Jake dismounted, trembling and out of breath.

Mrs. Skeffington, the old battle-ax of an Army wife, came bustling forward. "Stand back, there. Stand back. Can't you see Mr. Combs is hurt? Give him air." She turned to her long-suffering servant. "Pablo, get some water."

"*Sí, Señora* Skeffington," the old Mexican said, and hurried off.

They laid Combs on the ground. Webb held his head. Jake knelt beside the frontiersman, but there was nothing anyone could do. The arrow was deep in Combs's neck.

Blood had spurted all over his buckskins; there was blood in his long gray beard.

Combs looked up at Jake. The pale blue eyes were dimming rapidly. "Sorry," he whispered. "Too bad . . . too bad we didn't get . . . San Francisco to . . . together." Then he gave a great sigh and fell silent.

Jake helped Webb lay the body down. He closed the eyes gently. Then he stood.

Essex and the other skirmishers had returned. Jake traded glances with the bearded ex-Navy man.

"What now?" Essex said.

Desperately, Jake tried to shake off the feeling of loss, the feeling of hopelessness that had descended upon him with the death of Israel Combs. He knew one thing that had to be done. "Circle the wagons," he said. "Get as much of the stock inside as you can."

Some of the men started to move.

"Hold on, Moran," said Tyler Hampton, riding up. "I'm in command now. I give the orders."

3

"Then order the wagons circled," Jake said. "The Comanches could be back any minute."

Hampton sat his bay gelding easily. His dark eyes looked down at Jake with contempt. Jake remembered how the big Carolinian had protested the hours that Combs had spent putting them through wagon-circling drill. "Let them come. So much the better. We'll teach them a lesson they won't soon forget. Unlike you and the late Mr. Combs, Moran, I'm not scared of those painted savages. Give me fifty Carolina Mounted Rifles, and, by God, I'll ride through every Indian west of the Mississippi."

"You'd be riding to your grave, then," Jake told him. "You may be doing it now if you don't circle these wagons. Do you want to end up like Combs?"

Hampton snorted. "Combs was a fool or unlucky, or both."

The dead frontiersman lay at Jake's feet, arrows in his neck and leg. Behind them, the farmer Cutter's seven-year-old daughter, Rachel, was sobbing with fear as her mother and Mrs. Boone, her widowed aunt, led her and her older brother, Richard, back to their wagon. The elder Cutters were in their mid-thirties, but they looked fifteen years older, testimony to the hard life they had led as East Texas pioneers. Cutter's terrier Sparky and Molyneaux's two English mastiffs were barking. Most of the emigrants were gathered around Jake and Hampton, while a few others stood guard nervously.

Dan Essex spoke up. The ex-Navy lieutenant was of medium height, with well-trimmed chestnut hair and beard. He was solidly built, and his skin was burned a deep mahogany from years spent in the Pacific. Beneath his peaked leather cap, his emerald green eyes projected extraordinary calm and capability. "Look here, Hampton, Jake knows this part of the world. He knows Indians, too. Perhaps we—"

"No. You signed articles, Essex. So did every man here. You'll do as I say. We're short of water. We can't sit here worrying about Indians. We have to push on."

Essex stiffened. The muscles in his square jaw worked. He didn't like being talked to in this way, but he took it. Hampton was now the legally chosen authority.

Jake looked around the rest of the group. The men from whom he might have expected help—old Grinstead, going west to start a new life, and Cutter—looked uneasy but kept silent. No one else—not the newspaperman, Webb, nor the dandy, Molyneaux, nor the five gray-jacketed young Argonauts who called themselves the "New York Gold Hunters Association"—evinced a desire to challenge Hampton's authority. Jake couldn't blame them. Unlike him, these men had paid fifty dollars a head to join the company. Hampton had made good their deficiencies in equipment, animals, and provisions, which they had to repay at a fixed rate of interest when they reached California. They did not want to anger a man to whom they owed money.

There was another reason for their silence. Hampton's five teamsters were armed to the teeth with revolvers and bowie knives, and they knew how to use them. A week out of San Antonio, one of these men, an Irish tough named Mannion, had beaten up a young photographer from Philadelphia named Sloane. Combs had disciplined Mannion when he found out, but the emigrants had gotten the message. Many of them were openly fearful of Hampton's men.

Jake was scared. God, why did Israel Combs have to be

the one who died? With Hampton in charge, they'd probably all be dead soon.

There was a thudding of hooves and a jingling of bridle bits as the rest of Hampton's mounted troop returned from the chase. They were led by Blade, a short muscular man who had been Hampton's overseer back in South Carolina.

"Well?" Hampton said.

"They're gone," Blade said, reining in. "We put a good scare into 'em."

"Yeah," laughed a big, bearded teamster named Redmond, "they run like niggers from a work bell. They prob'ly won't stop till they get to Canada."

Hampton nodded. "No more than I expected. All right, we'll bury Combs and move on. As of now, Mr. Blade is my chief scout and hunter. Mr. McWilliams will be his assistant." McWilliams was a buckskin-clad teamster whom everyone knew as the Texas Ranger. Actually he'd been in the Militia—the Rangers had been disbanded in '48—but a lot of militiamen called themselves Rangers because it sounded more impressive.

Hampton turned, and a grin played along his thick lips. "Moran, I've never liked freeloaders. If we weren't so far from civilization, I'd set you on your own. As for your supposed new route to California, we'll try to find a scout who knows the way when we get to Coons Ranch. If not, we'll take the old route through Mexico. I'll let you ride rear guard for the rest of the trip, behind the cattle herd."

Jake tingled with anger and fear. He'd tried to keep away from Hampton, tried to avoid trouble with him. The two men had disliked each other at first sight, and nothing could change that. Everyone knew why Jake was being demoted. Hampton was determined to break him, to humiliate him. Jake forced himself to seem cool. He smiled back. "You're the captain."

"That's right, and don't forget it."

Hampton smiled again. He couldn't help himself. He'd gotten what he wanted—control of the company. He was the type who always had to be in charge. Combs had told Jake how enraged the Carolinian had been when he had lost the election for train captain. He had blamed the defeat on the Northerners in the company, since he was from a hotbed of slavery, when the truth was that the company was smart enough to put their trust in a man who knew the country.

"Let's get moving," Hampton said. He wheeled his big horse and rode off.

The gathering broke up. Some of the men, like Molyneaux and Webb, gave Jake sympathetic looks as they passed. The Englishman, Woodhouse, paused to say, "Bad luck, old boy." Woodhouse was in his early thirties. He was a naturalist who'd come on the expedition to gather specimens and make sketches for a book on the birds and quadrupeds of North America. He was slender and urbane, with uncallused hands. Besides the rakishly cocked silk hat, he wore a wine-colored coat, buff trousers, and two-tone riding boots. His sunburned nose and pink cheeks were peeling. He'd originally sported a pencil-thin mustache, but like everyone else he'd given up shaving when water got scarce.

Dan Essex said, "For what it's worth, Jake, I agree with you about the Indians." He smiled and added, "I just hope to hell we're wrong."

"You ain't the only one," Jake said.

Jake and the slave, Culpepper, dug a grave, and the company buried Israel Combs. Hampton read a psalm without emotion, and the company sang "Rock of Ages." After two and a half weeks of camping out, the men all looked alike—bearded and unwashed, their clothes torn and faded. The women were just as bedraggled, save for Mrs. Skeffington, whose bluish-gray hair seemed to have been sculpted in place, and whose dress was still as crisp and starched as her personality. Colonel Skeffington had been commander of the Military Department of Texas. When the commander of the San Francisco Presidio had suddenly died, Colonel Skeffington had been rushed west to take charge of that important post. His wife was following with their baggage and household goods.

The funeral was over quickly. Then the long, two-handed bullwhips and the shorter muleskinners' whips cracked, and the prairie reverberated with cries of "Stretch out!" and "Gee! Gee!" The scouts rode out, and the wagons lumbered into motion.

Hampton's two wagons led the way, followed by Mrs. Skeffington's Army wagon, then the rest. Each one passed over Combs's grave, obliterating it so that the body would not be found and mutilated by Indians. Most of the wagons were of medium or light weight, all that was practical for such a difficult journey—Cutter's was little more than a cart with a canvas top. Half were drawn by mules, half by oxen. Bringing up the rear was the giant Murphy wagon of the New York Gold Hunters Association, a modified Conestoga, looking patriotic with its red wheels, blue bed, and white top with the name painted in red letters. Besides their personal belongings and provisions, the Argonauts were carrying a five-story-tall gold and gem separator, whose graded tiers of sieves, when assembled, were supposedly capable of sifting everything from the largest nuggets to the finest dust.

Following the wagons came the horse herd, then the mules, then the cattle. At the rear of the cattle came Jake. Jake had left his wounded horse with the slave, Culpepper, and gotten a fresh mount from the *caballado*. The dust of the column drifted back onto him, choking him, filling his eyes. He tied his long bandana across his nose and mouth. He rode from side to side of the herd, chasing strays, urging stragglers along. It was hard work for man and horse. In addition, he constantly peered through the thick dust for the return of the Comanches.

Hampton's scouts reported no sign of the Indians. They were out there, though, Jake was sure of it. He wondered how many there were. At Fort Clark, the emigrants had crossed one of the great Comanche war trails leading into Mexico. Jake knew they were not far from another. He knew—because Combs had told him—that the Indians sometimes set up base camps in South Texas from which to launch their raids. Had the Indians who had attacked them been heading for one of those camps? Was the wagon train pointed straight for a giant war party?

On and on they marched, through the mid-morning heat. This route was called the Lower Road, but it was not a road as such. There were only the dim ruts of earlier wagon trains to show the way. The route was not as heavily traveled as before. Five years after the first great rush, men still flocked to California, but their numbers were declining. There was still gold to be found, but the old placer days were pretty much gone. Most of the mining work had been taken over by giant companies, employing hundreds of men, using expensive machinery and giant pressure hoses to scour the hillsides. There was still the odd fortune to be made, though, still gold enough to fuel the dreams of men who headed west and called themselves Argonauts.

Jake smiled. He had called himself an Argonaut once. It seemed like a long time ago. It was hard to remember those innocent times, with all that had happened since.

The sun rose higher. Men and animals plodded along. The featureless landscape looked like some fiend's conception of Hell. The sun seemed to have burned the life out of it. Despite the bandana, Jake's throat and nose were dry and caked with gritty dust, making it hard to breathe. The cattle were lowing with thirst. The Eastern blood cows, so fat at the start of the journey, were gaunt. They were having a tough go. The stringy Mexican longhorns, however, seemed to thrive in this land. They ate the dried bunch grass with alacrity, and they could go a long time without water.

The column had become dangerously strung out. The mule-drawn wagons had pulled ahead, leaving a gap in the lines. The horse herd was just passing a low ridge of sandy hills to the right when, through the cloud of dust, Jake saw movement.

Even as he drew aside to take a better look, a small party of Indians dashed from the cover of the hills, yelling and waving blankets and heading for the horses.

4

Jake drew a revolver and fired two warning shots, not caring as the tired, thirsty cattle broke into a lumbering stampede around him.

The Comanches paid no attention to Jake or the cattle. They bore down on the horse herd. Their yells made Jake's blood go cold. Up ahead, the horse wrangler, an Alabama boy named Bobby Durham, hesitated a second, and that second was his undoing. When at last he fired a wild shot and set his horse to run for the wagons, it was too late.

The frightened horse herd broke, and the blanket-waving Comanches bunched them up and steered them toward a low rise on the left, without seeming to miss a beat of their galloping pace. Jake watched helplessly as a heavyset Comanche with his horse painted red bore down on Bobby from behind. Bobby looked over his shoulder, terror on his bearded face. The Comanche caught him and drove his long feathered lance through Bobby's back, spitting him, lifting him off his horse and throwing him into the dust.

Red Horse leaped from his mount. He pulled his lance from Bobby's body, then he bent over the unfortunate Alabaman, drew his knife, and scalped him. Two more Indians joined in, hacking at Bobby's body, stripping it. Jake replaced his revolver and drew his rifle. He fired twice at the Indians, but his horse was unsteady and his shots missed. He did not charge. He didn't have the courage. He didn't want to die like Bobby. There were shouts from the wagons, and white riders appeared through the dust. The three Indians vaulted onto their mounts and rode away yelling, following the stolen horses. Red Horse waved Bobby's bloody scalp in triumph.

Jake watched them go. He was shaking violently. Sweat poured out of him. He smelled a rank odor and realized it was his own fear. The Comanches could have killed him, too. If they hadn't wanted horses more than scalps, he would be lying in the dust like Bobby Durham.

He rode forward, not wanting to. Bobby was naked. In that short space of time, the Indians had stripped him of all clothing and possessions, save for his socks. Their knives had slashed his pale body almost beyond recognition. Jake forced himself not to look. He was crying and shaking harder than ever and wishing to goddamn hell that Israel Combs was still alive.

The pounding hooves grew louder, and Tyler Hampton rode up, followed by a column of men. In the lead, Jake saw the Texas Ranger McWilliams, Essex, Woodhouse, and Jim Hart, the red-haired, athletic leader of the New York Argonauts.

Hampton reined in. His thick black brows were knit in anger. "What the hell happened?" he demanded, as if Durham's death and the loss of the horses were Jake's fault.

Jake recovered some of his composure. "What do you think happened?" he snapped. "Your Indians came back from Canada."

George Lambert and Ethan Andrews, the other Alabama boys, threw themselves from their horses. "Jesus Christ!" Ethan screamed when he saw what was left of his friend, and he began cursing insanely. Lambert was bent double near the mutilated body, retching and crying.

Blade, the muscular ex-overseer, rode up close to Jake. "Moran, what were you doing back here? Why didn't you stop—?"

"We'll attend to Moran later," Hampton said grimly.

"After we get the horses back." He looked around. "I'll take the best riders with me. Mannion!"

"Yeah, Cap'n?" called the Irishman.

"You're in charge here. Take old Grinstead, your friend the photographer, Willinsky, Nowak, that clerk Reed, and the old lady's Mexican. Round up the cattle and any horses you can find."

"Circle the wagons?" Jake said acidly.

"Yes, goddamn your eyes, circle the wagons, too. The rest of us will—"

"They're coming back!" The big teamster Redmond was galloping down from the rise. "It's the whole war party this time."

Hampton's dark eyes gleamed. "Dismount!" he shouted. "Form a firing line. We'll give the bastards a warm reception. Webb, you and Moran hold the horses."

The men drew their rifles and formed a rough line, some kneeling, some standing. Jake and the bespectacled newspaperman Webb gathered the horses safely behind. Jake knew he was supposed to be insulted at being a horse holder, but he was beyond caring.

The sound of hoofbeats grew loud. The emigrants saw dust. Then some two dozen Comanches came boiling over the low rise. They were yelling, brandishing lances, bows, and rifles. They came to an abrupt halt, as if surprised to see so many whites waiting for them.

"Now, men!" shouted Hampton. "Let 'em have it!"

The white men opened fire. They were yelling, too, from fear and hatred and a desire to revenge their mutilated companion. The boom of rifles contrasted with the sharp crack of carbines and the pop of revolvers. The Comanches rode back and forth. Those that had firearms traded shots with Hampton's men. They weren't close enough to use their powerful bows. Jake saw that their leader had shaved a large patch out of his long black hair. Hadn't Combs once said that was a sign of mourning?

The firing went on for several minutes. Acrid powder

smoke drifted over the line of white men. No one was hit on either side. Then the Indian leader yelled and waved his lance. As one man, the war party turned and rode away.

"They're running!" yelled Blade.

Hampton waved his rifle. "All right, Mannion, you know what to do. The rest of you men, mount up. Let's go after them!"

Fired with victory, the men scrambled for their horses. Jake mounted quickly. He rode ahead of the little group and wheeled his horse in front of Hampton, making Hampton pull his bay gelding up short.

"What the—?" Hampton began, lips drawn back in anger.

"Don't chase them," Jake warned. "That's what they want you to do. That attack, then the retreat—it's a trick. They're going to ambush you."

There was a murmur from the men. Hampton glared at Jake, breathing heavily. "We're going to get our horses back, Moran, and we're going to give those red bastards what they gave—or what you let them give—Durham. You can come, too." He smiled wickedly, "Unless, of course, you're yellow."

Jake stiffened in the saddle. He felt all eyes upon him. He knew that these men were riding into terrible danger, but after all that Israel Combs had said about him—about the Hero of Chapultapec and the companion of Sheriff Jack Hays—could he let them think he was a coward? Could he let them know the truth?

He yanked his horse's reins. "Let's go," he said.

5

The little force galloped over the rise in pursuit of the Comanches. They saw the two dozen Indians of the war party fleeing southward. Farther ahead, a large dust cloud revealed the location of the stolen horse herd.

"There they are, men!" Hampton yelled. "After them!"

The white men dug in their heels. They began closing the gap. Hampton was in the lead with Langdon Molyneaux, who rode a chestnut thoroughbred valued at $4,000. They were followed by Blade and the Texas Ranger, with the rest of the men strung out behind. They were hurrahing, thirsting to revenge Bobby Durham, filled with the sheer exhilaration of the chase. Jake hung back in the middle of the pack, sensing that the Comanches were going too slowly, expecting trouble.

They covered a mile of ground before they knew it. Closer and closer they came to the retreating Indians. The leading whites drew their revolvers and opened fire, cheering. Jake did not shoot. He wanted to save his ammunition. He had a feeling he'd need it later. He wished he'd reloaded the two chambers he'd fired previously. He carried spare revolver cylinders in his saddlebags, and he wished he had stuffed them in his flannel shirt, where he could get them in a hurry.

As Hampton's men opened fire, the Indians began drawing away again. Hampton spurred his mount recklessly in his desire to catch them. Others lathered their horses with reins or hats or even revolver barrels. From the corner of his eye, Jake saw Dan Essex drop out of the chase with a lamed horse.

Another mile flew by. Again the white men closed. Again they opened fire. Again the Indians drew away, and the whites yelled with frustration and blood lust, spurring their horses harder. Jake twisted his head anxiously to the sides and rear, praying they would not be surrounded.

Another mile. The men were well spread out by now. Ahead, the Indians were following the horse herd into a sort of natural funnel formed by two low ridge lines. Hampton waved his revolver and yelled. The cry was distorted by the thunderous pounding of hooves, but it sounded like "We've got them now!"

Then, on one of the ridge lines, Jake saw what he had dreaded—the glint of sunlight off metal.

"Stop!" he yelled, pointing. "Stop, it's a trap!" But no one heard.

Jake wanted to turn and run. He wanted to save himself. The Hero of Chapultapec couldn't do that, though. He wished he could.

He dug in his spurs, urging his mustang forward. He moved past red-haired Jim Hart, past Blade and the Texas Ranger. He moved past Molyneaux and drew even with Hampton. He yelled, nearly crying with frustration, but Hampton paid no attention.

He edged his horse closer to Hampton's, forcing it over. Hampton looked at him, swearing. All they needed was to have a collision, with both mounts tumbling to the ground injured. Jake waved. "Stop, you stupid son of a bitch! Stop!" Hampton paid no heed. Desperately, Jake forged ahead. He reached over and yanked one of the reins from Hampton's hand, almost pulling the big Carolinian out of the saddle. Hampton was incredulous. Jake wheeled his horse sharply to the right, forcing Hampton's to do the same. Behind them, the others slowed or turned to avoid hitting them.

Jake brought his horse to a stop. He let go Hampton's

rein. All around him was confusion, as men and horses slowed and milled and shouted. The horses were blowing.

"Look!" Jake screamed hoarsely, pointing to the ridge line. Hampton looked. So did the others. They saw nothing.

Hampton was furious. He pointed his revolver at Jake, thumbing back the hammer. "You cowardly—"

Then, as if in answer to Jake's prayers, the fleeing Indians ahead of them stopped and turned. The white men saw dust, and long lines of Indians suddenly materialized on two ridges. There must have been a hundred of them; they were less than a mile away. When they had seen the white men stop, they must have thought their ambush had been discovered.

For a moment, Hampton's men were too surprised and tired to comprehend what was happening.

"Get out of here!" Jake yelled.

The men wavered. They seemed mesmerized by the sight of so many Indians, and by the realization of how close they had come to being trapped. Some of them looked at Hampton, but he was still staring at the Indians, as if he couldn't believe that all his assumptions had been wrong.

The Indians were moving off the ridge. "Go!" yelled Jake. "Goddamn it, go!" He began beating at the horses with his hat.

Suddenly, as if something collectively snapped, the men turned their mounts. They kicked them and whipped them with their reins. Molyneaux sprinted off on his $4,000 thoroughbred. Hampton was still staring. "Come on, Cap'n," said the overseer, Blade, tugging Hampton's coat sleeve. "We can't fight that many."

Hampton still hesitated, but Blade rode off. Loyalty was forgotten in the desire to save his scalp. Jake was already at a gallop when he saw Hampton turn, finally coming out of his trance.

The men raced for the distant wagons. It was a free-for-all now, and the devil take the hindmost. Exhilaration had turned to fear. Ahead of him, Jake saw the gray-haired Cutter throw away his pistol in his haste to escape.

Behind them the air erupted with howling yells as the Comanches took up the chase. Gunshots sounded from the ridges. Jake had drawn ahead of everyone save Webb, who'd been bringing up the rear before the turnabout. Suddenly Jake's horse missed stride. He stumbled, recovered, and went on. He'd been hit. At that extreme range, it had been the luckiest of shots, probably from a captured Sharps. Jake swore wildly, cursing his luck. He prayed to God at the same time, because he knew that if his horse couldn't make it to the wagons, he would die.

The Indians were in full cry behind them, gaining steadily. They weren't pretending to go slowly now. Combs had once told Jake that trying to outrun Comanches was suicide, because they were the best horsemen in the world. There was no choice, though. There was no place to fort up till they reached the wagons. They couldn't afford to get surrounded in the open.

More gunshots, more hideous yells. Jake glanced back. The big teamster, Redmond, the one who'd made the joke about the Indians running to Canada, was far in the rear. His horse was slowing, beat from carrying its heavy load. Redmond was screaming in terror. Jake saw the big man suddenly reel in the saddle, then fall off. Jake hoped for his sake that he was dead.

Jake turned back and put his head low to the mustang's lathered neck, praying that the horse would last a little longer, feeling the animal's heart beating fast and irregularly, knowing that he was nearly played out. Poor damn animal. It wasn't his fight.

He was falling back in the pack now. He saw the looks he was getting from the scared men—from Blade, from the Englishman Woodhouse, from George Lambert. They were looks of admiration—Christ, they thought he was dropping back to cover their retreat! His horse's wound was deep; there wasn't much blood to see.

He dug his spurs into the dying animal's flanks and whipped him brutally with his reins. The horse's gait was becoming unsteady. Jake caught a few last glances as more whites passed him—Ethan Andrews and Blade. They thought he was being a hero. "Wait!" he cried, but the word stuck in his cracked throat, and they did not hear.

There was a shallow depression ahead. The little horse made it down one steep side and labored up the other, but that last effort took too much out of him. He slowed clumsily, his legs flailing out of stride. Then he stopped altogether, blowing heavily, head down.

Frantically Jake whipped the beast, crying, pleading. He didn't want to die. He could hear the Comanches yelling behind him. The horse was white with lather. There was bloody foam at his mouth. His eyes rolled up in his head, and his legs were unsteady.

Jake dismounted. All his companions were gone. All save one, who was just coming up the far side of the depression, heading right for Jake.

Tyler Hampton.

Jake moved away from the dying horse. He braced himself, ready to grab an extended arm and swing up behind Hampton. He'd seen it done before, but he'd never tried it himself. It was hard to do with a fast-moving horse, and he prayed to God he could pull it off.

Jake expected Hampton to slow down, but he didn't. The Carolinian swerved away from where Jake waited. He looked Jake full in the eye as he galloped past, and Jake saw a malicious smile. Then he was gone, riding for the wagons.

"Wait, you bastard!" Jake cried, turning. "You son of a—!" He drew his revolver and aimed it at Hampton's retreating back. Then he lowered it. He couldn't do that, not even to Tyler Hampton.

The Indian yells were loud in his ears. He heard shots again, and something kicked up dirt nearby. He pulled his horse to the ground and onto its side. He wanted to shoot the animal, but each bullet was precious now. In the few seconds remaining to him, he took cover behind the dying horse. He drew his Sharps rifle and a handful of cartridges and laid them on the saddle. He laid his revolvers there, too, with the spare cylinders from the saddlebags. He intended to sell his life as dearly as possible. He would save one bullet for himself, though. He would kill himself rather than become a prisoner.

6

The hoofbeats were a continuous, swelling roar, like the approach of some terrible storm. The yelling Comanches were pouring across the plain. Hastily, inexpertly, Jake practiced for the final moment. He tried a pistol in different positions, found that upside down was easiest. That way he could flip it quickly into his mouth and pull the trigger.

The first breechclouted riders began charging out of the depression. Jake laid the rifle barrel across the saddle. He smelled the worn leather of the saddle, smelled the sour sweat of the horse and the hot blood from the horse's wound. He drew a bead on the lead rider—it looked like the chief, the one with the mourning patch shaved out of his hair. He held his fire.

The Indians rode straight at him, then they broke to the sides, going around and meeting again, forming their famous circle. They didn't fire. Neither did Jake. Something told him to wait for them to make the first move.

They rode around him, yelling like fiends from Hell. He shifted, trying to look in every direction at once. He expected an attack from his unprotected rear. But they held off. No arrows came his way, no bullets. His wounded horse struggled to rise, but Jake forced him back down.

He watched the Indians across his rifle barrel, admiring their barbaric splendor. The leader was Chief Patch, all right; Jake saw the shaven spot clearly now. He saw Red Horse, as well, with Bobby Durham's scalp waving from his long lance. He saw painted faces and bodies. He saw shaggy horses, many with their legs painted with white clay, red ribbons streaming from their tails. He saw more scalps hanging from feathered shields and bridles. The Indians slung themselves from side to side on their horses' backs, showing off, yelling and waving their weapons out of sheer pleasure. Their long black hair blew free, and their squat bodies seemed as one with those of their animals.

Jake kept his finger poised on the trigger, waiting, waiting. What were they doing? Why didn't they come after him and be done with it? Was this some kind of mental torture? If so, it was a good one. They circled and circled, and the dust and the yelling and the pounding hooves were driving him mad. The earth trembled beneath him; he could scarcely breathe the thick air.

All at once, they stopped.

There was no word of command. They acted as if they were of one mind, a hundred components of the same organism. It was a brilliant piece of horsemanship. One moment they were at a full gallop; the next, they sat their horses calmly, while the great cloud of dust blew slowly away.

Then the dust was gone. A hundred savages were quietly watching Jake. A hundred pairs of eyes bored into him. He wiped his dry mouth with the back of his scarred hand. He tried not to show fear. Somehow that seemed important, even though he was trembling so badly he thought they must see it.

He watched the chief, the one with the patch shaved from his long hair. The chief walked his horse slowly forward. His face was painted with black war stripes, red stripes adorned his arms and chest, and there were tattooed designs around his old battle scars. His copper-colored body looked compact and explosively powerful. He was older than most Comanche warriors, proud and majestic, with a sure sense of himself. A blond scalp ornamented his horse's bridle. Jake shivered—his own scalp might be there next.

Jake could have shot the chief, but he didn't. He didn't know why. Too scared to act, maybe.

From his horse, Patch looked down at Jake. Jake made himself stare back. Behind the Indian's dark eyes was—what? Something unfathomable, some form of reasoning no white man could understand. Jake's throat was so dry and cracked that it hurt. His breathing was rapid as a bellows; his heart pounded loudly in his chest. Sweat poured down his face, it made his hands slippery on his rifle.

With a movement so abrupt that it startled Jake, Patch raised his long lance and yelled something at him. Jake forced himself to keep staring at the Indian; he forced himself not to move. Then the Comanche chief turned and yelled to his followers. The Indians raised their weapons, and they all gave a great shout together. Then, again as one, they wheeled their ponies and rode away.

Jake could hardly believe what was happening. The drumming of hoofbeats receded in a vast cloud of dust as the Comanches vanished into the west. The dust drifted down on Jake; it settled over him, filling his eyes with grit. He half expected the Comanches to reappear out of it, but they didn't.

He waited, barely breathing. Was it a trick? Some new way of inflicting mental anguish on him? Were they really gone?

Yes.

Jake collapsed across the saddle limply, like a rag doll. He could scarcely control his trembling body.

Why? Why had they done it?

Maybe they hadn't known his horse was hit, and they had admired what they had thought was his bravery in facing them alone. Maybe, like so many whites, they thought he was some kind of hero. Jake remembered the look in Patch's eyes; he would remember that look to his dying day. The proud old Indian had held Jake's life in the palm of his hand, and he had given it back. After trying so hard to kill him. Indian ways were mysterious. Who understood them?

Jake lay across his saddle for a while; he didn't know how long. His eyes were closed; his breath was shallow. Flies buzzed on his face and around the horse's wound. The hot sun beat down. He drifted in and out of consciousness, like a man in fever; like a dead man coming back to life.

At last he struggled to his feet. Irregular shudders rent the horse's body. A weak hoof pawed occasionally at the ground. One big eye followed Jake, imploring him. Jake cocked his revolver and put a bullet in the horse's brain.

He holstered his revolvers. Then he unlooped his canteen from the saddle. He started to take a deep drink, stopped, and sipped instead. Water was more precious than gold right now. He rolled the cooling liquid around in his mouth, then let it slip down his parched throat. He slung the canteen over his shoulder, along with his saddlebags. He picked up his rifle and started walking back to the wagons.

He wondered if the wagons had moved on, or if they were still circled. If they were gone, he was lost. It was hard to tell what they had done, with a man like Tyler Hampton in charge.

Hampton. What was he going to do about Hampton? A real man would call Hampton out for leaving him that way. A real man would make Hampton pull his pistols and shoot it out until one of them was dead. Jake swallowed painfully in his cracked throat. He would not do that, not if there was any way around it. He was too afraid that he would be the one who died. Dan Essex wouldn't be afraid, he thought bitterly, nor would Israel Combs have been. His late brother, Ben, certainly wouldn't have been afraid. Jake cursed his own cowardice and his feelings of inadequacy.

He stumbled along, now and then glancing fearfully over his shoulder, still half expecting the Comanches to return. He doubted that they would let him live a second time.

Then, through the heat haze, he saw movement to his front. Horsemen.

He stopped. His shoulders sagged. He should have known his escape was too good to be true. The horsemen were turning toward him; they must have seen him. There was nowhere to run, nowhere to take cover. He hadn't the strength left to fight them; he hadn't the strength to raise his rifle. He drew one of his revolvers. Better to kill himself quickly and get it over with.

The horsemen were coming at a brisk canter now. He cocked the revolver.

"Jake?"

He hesitated. His head was swimming.

"Jake, is that you?" It sounded like Dan Essex.

Jake squinted his eyes, trying to focus against his tears and the sun's glare. The horsemen rounded into view. They were white. There was Essex at their head; Jake recognized the trim beard and peaked leather cap. Behind him were Woodhouse and Cutter, Hart, the Texas Ranger, Ethan Andrews, and the slave, Culpepper.

Jake stood there, watching them stupidly, the cocked revolver at his side, as they rode up to him.

"Jake!" cried Essex. "My God, you're alive!"

7

Jake had to put on an act. He had to be the man they thought he was. He holstered the revolver and wiped his eyes surreptitiously with his sleeve, as though he were wiping sweat from his brow. "God had a lot to do with it, believe me," he said, grinning.

The rescue party gathered around. Somebody passed Jake a canteen, and he drank. "How did you do it?" Essex marveled. "My horse went lame during the chase, and I had to walk back to the wagons. The others caught up to me, and I heard how you'd stayed behind to cover them. When the Indians failed to attack us, I got a new horse and some volunteers, and we came to . . . well, frankly, we came to recover your body. Hampton didn't want us to go, but after the courage you showed, we couldn't just leave you out here."

A smile broadened the ex-Navy man's tanned face. "And here you are alive. I'm glad, damned glad."

"I'm pretty glad myself," Jake said. He took another sip of water. "But it wasn't because of anything I did."

"Sure it wasn't." Red-haired Jim Hart, the Harvard boy, grinned.

"How many'd you git?" the Ranger, McWilliams, asked. He fingered the shotgun he carried across his saddle.

Jake shook his head. "Only shot I fired was to put down my horse."

That remark provoked knowing grins and laughter. Jake tried to explain what had happened. He tried to explain

41

about his wounded horse, and about Chief Patch and the look in his dark eyes, but these men didn't want to hear.

"You're being too modest about your accomplishments, old boy," said the Englishman, Woodhouse, smiling through his sunburn. "One can carry the reluctant hero's role too far, you know."

"The battle must have been as impressive as your exploits at Chapultepec," Hart added. "I feel absolutely terrible about running away. You've shamed us all, Captain Moran."

Jake said, "I didn't shame nobody. I—"

"Must've been some shootin', to drive off a passel like that," observed the dour farmer Cutter. "Reckon you're 'bout as good as ole Combs said you was."

"Better, mebbe," McWilliams said.

"Course we didn't hear but the one shot," said Ethan Andrews thoughtfully. Ethan was a sharp lad of nineteen, with an unruly mop of dark hair. He was going to California in hopes of finding enough gold to pay off his family's debts and see his sisters well married.

"Sound plays funny tricks in the desert," Essex explained to the young man. "It's the same at sea. Remember, the breeze was blowing away from us."

"I'd surely like to go back and count up the bodies," Cutter said.

McWilliams shook his head. "Like as not, we wouldn't find nothin'. Comanches carry off their dead." He spat contemptuously in the direction where the Indians had disappeared.

"Let's get out of here before they come back and carry us off," Jake said.

The slave Culpepper was leading the spare horse, originally intended for Jake's body. He held the reins while Jake mounted. "Surprised Langdon let you out of his sight," Jake joked. Runaway slaves were Molyneaux's pet fear. "Weren't you worried about the Indians?"

Culpepper looked emotionless under his glazed hat. "I

don't care 'bout no Indians. For me, this is a few minutes of freedom."

The party turned their horses and started across the dusty plain for the wagons. They sat lightly in their saddles, keeping their eyes peeled for renewed trouble.

"While we were off chasing that bunch, another party of Comanches hit the wagons," Essex informed Jake.

"Anybody hurt?"

"Mannion's dead. So's Pablo."

Jake thought of Mrs. Skeffington without her servant, Pablo. How would the old harridan hold her afternoon teas now?

"Anybody else?" he said.

"Grinstead was creased in the head, but he'll be all right. Nowak took an arrow in the shoulder. That's not all, though. They got most of the spare mules and all our cattle."

That meant there was no food, save what was in the wagons and what they could hunt up in the way of game. It meant there were no relief teams if some of the draft animals should die or pull up lame.

Essex went on, upset. "Our best horses are half dead with fatigue, and there's hardly any water. None of this should have happened. None of it."

Essex's words were a none-too-subtle indictment of Tyler Hampton. A few of the men cast glances at McWilliams, but the buckskin-clad Ranger said nothing in defense of his employer. He had other things on his mind.

Jake didn't like the craggy-faced McWilliams, but he could sympathize with him. McWilliams had originally farmed a headright in Llano County with his brother and family. Then one day, while he was away at the fields, Comanches had struck. He'd come home to find his brother scalped and carved apart. His wife had been raped, scalped, and shot through with arrows. The Comanches had carried off his two girls, aged eight and three. The eight-year-old had been found on the trail, raped and bleeding to death.

The three-year-old was never recovered. She had disappeared into the vastness of Comancheria, to a childhood of brutality and slavery and—if she lived that long—to adulthood as the wife of a Comanche warrior. Something had snapped in McWilliams's mind. He had given up the farm and joined the Militia. He wanted to kill Indians, any Indians, and the Militia wasn't particular. When they couldn't find Comanches—and they usually couldn't—they had attacked peaceful Tonkawas and Kickapoos, slaughtering men, women, and children until even McWilliams had had enough blood on his hands. He wanted to get away from Texas, to get away from his terrible memories; and if that meant being a hired gun for Tyler Hampton, so be it. The Indian wars had come back to him with a vengeance now, though, and his eyes held a mad gleam.

The party had jogged a long mile across the prairie. Ahead they saw a mounted sentry. It was Ross, another of Hampton's men. The black-bearded Missourian stood in his stirrups as the party came on. "Holy Christ," he said when he saw Jake. He turned and shouted down the low rise, "Moran's alive!"

Ross stared at Jake as at Lazarus risen from the dead, openmouthed, with his gold front tooth showing. He started to follow the party. "Stay here," Essex told him sharply. "You're on duty."

The men rode down the rise toward the circled wagons. The surviving animals were scattered outside, grazing on what grass they could find. There was another mounted lookout to the east; it looked like George Lambert.

Ross's cry had alerted the emigrants, and they came piling out of the wagons to escort the rescue party in. They swarmed around Jake, pounding his legs and back like he was the greatest hero since George Washington, shouting and asking what had happened.

"Jake drove them Comanches off all by hisself," Cutter told them. "Kilt him I don't know how many."

"If it hadn't been for his stand, we'd likely all be dead now," Jim Hart said.

Once again, Jake tried to tell the truth, but he finally gave up. Nobody listened to him. Nobody wanted to hear. After the day's disasters, the emigrants *wanted* to believe that Jake had performed mighty deeds against the Indians. The thought gave them comfort and hope. Even Hampton's overseer, Blade, was staring at him with something resembling admiration.

They passed through the circle of wagons with everybody talking at once; and every time the story was repeated, the toll of Indians from Jake's deadly six-shooters mounted. Jake saw spent arrows on the ground and sticking in the wagons. Some of the animals were wounded. There was old Grinstead with his head bandaged. There was the fiercely mustachioed Nowak with his right arm in a sling. As a student, Nowak had battled the Austrians across the Prague barricades during the revolution of '48. Forced to flee his native land, he'd arrived in New York with little more than his violin. To earn a living, he'd formed an orchestra, and he had become well known playing waltzes by, ironically, Austrians like Lanner and the Strauss family.

Off by themselves were three objects covered by canvas shrouds.

Mrs. Skeffington came up to Jake, every silver-blue hair in place. Only her blood-spattered dress gave evidence she'd been in a battle—she had probably removed the arrow from Nowak's shoulder. "You did well, young man," she said. "We're proud of you. Would you like me to make you some tea?"

Jake grinned. "I'd rather have whiskey, ma'am, if it's all the same with you."

There was hearty laughter.

Mrs. Skeffington said, "I've some brandy in the wagon. Would that do?"

"Yes, ma'am. Thank you."

Mrs. Skeffington bustled off, and Jake dismounted. Suddenly Tyler Hampton was standing before him. The two men stared at each other.

"Hello, Hampton," Jake said.

"Hello, Moran. Made it back, I see." A little grin played around the Carolinian's fleshy lips. Jake wished he had the guts to bash in the big man's face. Apparently no one had seen Hampton abandon him; no one was crying out for Jake to settle his debt of honor. Jake was not going to mention the incident. He was too scared. He and Hampton would keep it their secret. Jake hated himself.

Mrs. Skeffington returned with a crystal decanter and a large snifter. She poured some brandy for Jake, who drank the fiery liquid in one gulp, feeling it steady his ragged nerves. He held out the empty snifter. The old woman raised her eyebrows, but she poured more.

Dan Essex had not joined in the congratulations. His anger seemed to be feeding on itself. He turned his horse loose to graze, and he mounted the tongue of the Argonauts' red-white-and-blue Conestoga, the most prominent wagon in the circle. On a jerry-built staff behind him flapped a green-and-white flag with the red letters "EXCELSIOR," a departure gift from the sisters of Jim Hart and the clerk Harvey Reed.

Essex raised a hand. "Order! Order!" he bawled. "Listen to me!" He had a deep, quarterdeck voice and the kind of personal magnetism that commanded attention.

The noise stopped. All heads turned.

Essex's normally calm eyes were narrowed; there was fire in them. He glared at Tyler Hampton from beneath his leather cap. Perhaps he had not forgotten the brusque treatment he'd received from Hampton earlier that day. He turned back, and his voice was cold. "Mr. Webb, you're secretary of this company. You will please note in the log that I've called the company to order, as is my privilege under the articles."

The bespectacled newspaperman looked uneasily from Essex to Hampton and nodded.

Essex went on, addressing the company. "Men, had we circled the wagons when Captain Moran advised, we'd not have lost our horse herd. Had we stayed put here instead of chasing Comanches, Pablo and Mannion would probably be alive now, and we'd still have our cattle. Besides Indians, we now face death from starvation and thirst. We'll be lucky to get out of this alive, any of us; and from where I stand, it's the fault of one person—Tyler Hampton."

"What are you saying?" snarled Hampton. He elbowed through the crowd, his burly head and shoulders pushed aggressively forward, trying to intimidate the ex-sailor.

Essex stared Hampton in the eye. Any man who'd gone aloft in a typhoon—and Essex had—was unlikely to be intimidated by Tyler Hampton. "I'm saying you're incompetent, sir. I'm saying you're not fit to lead this company."

A murmur went through the crowd. Hampton straightened; violent anger ranged across his dark features.

Essex went on. "I'm calling for an election. I'm calling for a new captain."

Everyone started talking at once. A lot of them agreed with Essex. They'd had enough of Hampton. Jake jolted down his brandy. He was more than ready to vote for Dan Essex as captain.

Hampton could barely control himself. "Who's going to replace me, Essex? You?"

"No. I nominate Jake Moran."

There was a roar of approval.

Jake dropped the brandy snifter, breaking it. "No, not me. You got the wrong man. Dan here should be the—"

"The devil we have the wrong man," Essex said. "You just stood off a hundred Comanches single-handedly. You're not the wrong man—not by a long shot."

Hampton turned on Jake. "So you're behind this, eh, Moran? I should have known." He stared at the company menacingly. "By our articles, you need a second for that nomination."

For a moment there was silence. Then Woodhouse spoke up. "I'll second it." He smiled insouciantly. "After all, we must observe form, mustn't we?"

Hampton bared his teeth, but before he could act, Jim Hart took a deep breath, "I'll second it, too."

"And me," said Cutter, chomping on a corncob pipe.

"And me, as well," Mrs. Skeffington said.

"You're a woman," snapped Hampton, "You've no rights here."

"I daresay I'm a better man than you are, sir," retorted the old lady haughtily. That drew laughter, which enraged Hampton all the more. Mrs. Skeffington went on. She spoke in a nasal, lecturing tone, head cocked slightly to one side, like a governess addressing her charges. "Perhaps I'm not allowed a vote under our company's constitution, but I wish everyone to know where I stand. Mr. Hampton has been a disappointment. There is no reason he should not be dismissed. I think Captain Moran would make an excellent choice for leader—even if he has broken one of my best brandy snifters."

There was more laughter and shouted approval.

Jake's heart sank. He waved his arms helplessly. This was a mistake. "No, I don't want the job. I won't take it. You people don't know—"

"No time for modesty, Jake," Essex said. "We need you. You're the one to get us through." He raised his voice to the back of the crowd. "Call in the sentries, please. We'll require their votes, as well."

Jake cursed every lie he'd ever let others believe about him. He couldn't take responsibility for the lives of these people. He wasn't qualified. He—

"You won't get away with this, Moran," Hampton said. His eyes were pinpoints of anger.

Jake made no reply.

"You've been angling to take over this wagon train from

the start. Well, this is my company. Any man that says it isn't, better be prepared to take the consequences.''

Yesterday that threat would have been enough to assure Hampton's reelection. Now, though, two of Hampton's hired thugs were dead, and the emigrants were so buoyed by Jake's miraculous survival against the Comanches that they had themselves believing he could walk on water.

"That's enough, Hampton," Essex said from the Argonauts' wagon. The sentries were in now; the company was fully assembled. "I will ask for a show of hands. Mr. Blade, I will ask you to verify my count, if you will be so kind. All those in favor of Tyler Hampton retaining his position as captain, please signify."

Blade's hand shot up, as did Ross's. McWilliams raised his, too, though Jake sensed reluctance. Slowly, Webb and Molyneaux raised their hands, as well. There were no others.

Essex counted the hands to himself. "Those for Jake Moran?"

The rest of the hands went up—Essex, Woodhouse, the five Argonauts, George Lambert and Ethan Andrews, old Grinstead, Cutter. Even those who owed the most money to Hampton defied him.

Essex counted silently once again. "I make it five for Hampton and eleven for Jake Moran. Are those your figures, Mr. Blade?"

The overseer nodded, looking at Hampton reluctantly. What else could he do?

Essex said, "Mr. Webb, you will so record it. Captain Moran is our new leader."

There was a whoop of celebration. Once again, people were pounding Jake's back. "Nothing can stop us now!" shouted George Lambert.

Hampton had gone white. The big Carolinian could not believe the turn of events. Deposed from command of his own company—and after less than a day in charge. The story would get out when they reached California; it was bound to. It would follow him everywhere; he would never escape it. People would laugh at him, and Tyler Hampton could not stand being laughed at. Politics, social prominence—all were suddenly lost to him now. He was ruined in California before he had even gotten there.

Jake felt like he was staring into a bottomless pit, preparing to be pushed in. He was not a leader; he was not a hero like these people believed. He wasn't fit to be their captain; he was going to get them all killed. God, why did it have to be him? Not only was he now responsible for the lives of every man, woman, and child in the company, but, as he watched Hampton's jaw working, he knew that he had made himself a deadly enemy, as well.

8

The emigrants stared at Jake expectantly, as though with one pronouncement he could end their troubles. Like it or not, they had chosen him. They were depending on him. He could not back out. One thing was clear—if he was going to be their leader, he had to lead. He had to act, to be decisive—or at least to appear that way. It was their only chance for survival.

He debated turning back for San Antonio, but it was a day and a half to the last water. They'd never make it. They had no choice but to push on. "McWilliams," he said, "take a fresh horse. Ride ahead and scout for water. Watch out for Indians."

"Stay where you are, McWilliams," Tyler Hampton said. The big Carolinian stared at Jake. "My men obey no orders of yours, Moran. Nor do I."

Jake rested his scarred hands on his hips. He had anticipated that Hampton would challenge him right away. He remembered what Combs had said about men like this. Inside the circle of wagons, it grew very quiet.

Jake said, "Then get out, Hampton. Now. Take those who want to go with you."

Hampton sneered at him, shifting his bulk confidently from one foot to the other. "You can't make me leave, and you can't make me take your orders."

Jake reached behind his back and pulled out one of his Navy Colts. He cocked it and pointed it at Hampton. "Yes, I can."

Before Hampton could react, Jake shifted the Colt to his left hand. He reached across his waist, pulled out the other Colt and cocked that, too. He stepped back, widening his field of fire, so that he covered Hampton and his three remaining men. Most of the emigrants hurried out of the way, fearful of stray bullets. Dan Essex stepped forward with his pistol drawn, taking a position alongside Jake.

"Thanks, Dan, but I can handle this," Jake said. That was the way it had to be. He had to do this himself.

Hampton recovered. His sneer became more pronounced. "What are you going to do, Moran? Kill me?"

Jake smiled grimly. "No, I'm going to shoot off your kneecaps."

Hampton's sneer crumbled as Jake went on, "I'm going to leave you here to crawl around in circles till you die of thirst, or till the buzzards peck out your eyes. Or maybe the Comanches will come back first—who knows?"

"You wouldn't do that," Hampton said.

"Try me."

They faced each other. Hampton's hate-filled eyes went from Jake's eyes to the octagonal barrels of Jake's Colts, then back again.

Jake prayed that Hampton didn't call his bluff. Jake had never shot a man in cold blood. He didn't think he could do it—he *knew* he couldn't do it. He wasn't even sure he'd be able to fire if Hampton and his men went for their guns. He hoped he looked like he wanted revenge for being abandoned on the prairie. He hoped he looked like he was just begging for an excuse to shoot.

At last Hampton let out his breath. "Let's go," he said to his men. "We'll push on by ourselves."

The muscular overseer Blade, who owed everything to Hampton, was ready to follow. The other two teamsters hesitated. "Well?" Hampton said.

McWilliams straightened. His eyes narrowed in his craggy face. "Four men alone won't stand much chance if we run into Comanches. Sorry, Mr. Hampton, but I reckon I'll stay with the wagons."

Ross scratched his unkempt black beard. Ross had killed a man in Missouri, and some said he was leaving Texas one step ahead of Judge Lynch. "The Ranger's right, boss. It'd be awful risky out there by ourselves."

"You're not coming, then?"

Ross shook his head, nervously, because he was afraid of his employer.

"Webb, Molyneaux—what about you?"

The New Orleans newspaperman licked his thin lips.

Molyneaux said, "Come on, Hampton. It was a fair election. Swallow your pride and come with us. You've no choice, you know."

Hampton's thick chest was heaving. Then he looked away. "I'll come," he said. He said it quickly, in a low voice.

Jake kept the cocked pistols trained. "You'll do more than that, Hampton. You'll follow orders. Right?"

No answer.

"Right?"

"Yes, all right," hissed Hampton savagely. He had given in—for now.

Jake lowered the revolver hammers and holstered the weapons. As Hampton stalked off, he seemed to feel a sigh of relief from the onlookers, but it was nothing compared with his own relief. He grinned, as though he did this sort of thing all the time. "Mrs. Skeffington, I'd be obliged for another drink of that brandy, ma'am."

"I'll fetch a new snifter," the gray-haired Army wife said.

"That won't be necessary." Jake took the crystal decanter from her and held it to his lips, taking a huge swallow of the warm, bracing liquid.

He wiped his mouth and returned the now half-empty decanter. "Thanks," he wheezed. He wished he could have drunk it all.

With his authority firmly established, at least for the moment, Jake said, "All right. McWilliams, head out. George, you and Ross slaughter the wounded cattle. Cut steaks off 'em, and we'll cook 'em tonight. Willinsky, you and Sloane gather up all these arrows and break 'em in half." He smashed a revolver barrel on an arrow sticking from the nearest wagon bed, shattering it by way of demonstration.

"Why do that?" Willinsky asked. He and Sloane were puzzled.

Jake worked the broken arrow from the wagon bed. It was made of ash, with owl feathers. There were four grooves carved along the shaft, two straight and two spiral, and the war head was made of barbed flint. "Takes a Comanche a long time to make one of these. First he's got to find the wood, then he shapes it and smoothes it, then he puts on the feathers and a head. It's a valuable piece of property to him. After we're gone, they'll be back for these. Every one we break is one less they can shoot at us later. Take the heads off and bury them."

Willinsky smiled with understanding. The Argonaut had once been fat, but two and a half weeks of heat, bad food, and dysentery had changed that, though it had not removed the innate good humor from his cherubic face. Frank Sloane, the photographer, nodded gravely. Sloane was the only one of the Argonauts who did not wear a gray jacket. He had joined the others on the steamer south from Philadelphia. He was headed west to get over a failed love affair.

"Get to work, then," Jake said. He heard hoofbeats as McWilliams rode out. He looked for Molyneaux's slave in the crowd. "Culpepper, get yourself a rifle and some pistols from the dead men."

That brought a murmur of unrest from the Southern members of the company. Hampton took note with a raised eyebrow. "See here, Jake," Molyneaux said, "aren't you going a bit far? That nigger's my property. You can't just—"

"We might be fighting for our lives in a little bit, Langdon. We'll need every gun we can get. It don't matter to me if the fella pulling the trigger is white, black, or has blue polka dots on his butt—'long as he can shoot Comanches.''

Molyneaux hesitated. With his beard and dusty clothes, his torn straw hat and twill trousers ripped out at the knees, he didn't look like a dandy now—he looked hardly better than his slave. He nodded reluctantly to Culpepper, who flashed a look at Jake and limped off. "Cut some meat off those oxen and save it for the dogs," Molyneaux called after him.

"Everybody else, lighten your wagons," Jake ordered. "Dump everything heavy, everything that ain't absolutely necessary for the trip. These animals have been thirty-six hours without water. They'll start lying down soon if we don't lighten their loads. And once they lie down, they won't get up again."

The emigrants hesitated. They had carried their possessions from their homes—two thousand miles, some of them. They'd intended to carry them all the way to California. It was hard to give these things up, hard to leave them to the sun and the wind and roving bands of Indians.

"Let's go," Jake said.

Still they wavered. Then Mrs. Skeffington stepped forward, "Well, come on, you people. We've no time to stand around moping. Captain Moran, help me empty this wagon, please. I cannot do heavy work any longer, and my servant is gone."

"Yes, ma'am," Jake said.

The first thing to go was a wooden box with her Sèvres tea service. Jake raised his eyebrows; he had some idea how much that was worth.

"Don't fiddle-faddle, young man. I've lost far worse than this in thirty years of following the flag." Next came a trunkful of clothes, then she started on the household goods.

Reluctantly, the other emigrants followed Mrs. Skeffington's lead. Soon the ground inside the circle of wagons was piled with tents and clothes and blankets, with kettles and furniture and half-kegs of nails. There was a plowshare from Cutter's wagon, the effects of the dead men, and old Grinstead's rocking chair. There were pigs of lead and tools of all description. There were spare axles and lumber and enough metal fittings to build another wagon. Jake was traveling with only the clothes on his back, but Mess Number 1, the wagon he shared with Essex and Woodhouse, contributed coats and boots and boxes of books. Essex threw in his old brass telescope. "I've had this since I was a midshipman," he said, and gave a sigh. "Oh, well." He tossed it on the pile.

When they were done, Jake went around the wagons, inspecting. "Webb, what about this printing press?"

"Please, Captain Moran, that press is my livelihood. Without it, I'm lost. I might as well leave myself here as leave my press. Please, it doesn't weigh that much."

Jake knew he should insist that the press be dumped. But the bespectacled little newspaperman looked so pathetic, so pleading, that Jake decided to give him a chance. "Very well. But if your animals die on you, don't expect us to provide you new ones."

He came to the New York Gold Hunters' red-white-and-blue Conestoga. Outside were clothes and books and useless implements—someone had even been carrying an astrolabe.

Jake glanced inside. "One thing more to go, I'm afraid."

The five young men looked among themselves. "The gold and gem separator?" the clerk Harvey Reed said at last.

Jake nodded. "It wouldn't have worked, anyway," he said quietly.

Harvey lowered his head. He was good-looking in an intellectual sort of way, but his beard was thin and scraggly, and it made his face break out, so that he was constantly scratching it. "Oh, well. It was . . . it was . . ."

"It was fun while it lasted," said Jim Hart, Harvey's lifelong neighbor and best friend.

Willinsky and Sloane and the wounded Nowak nodded. The day's events had shaken their boyish enthusiasm. They had grown up. Newspapers and books had made them think crossing the prairie and fighting Indians would be a lark. Now they had experienced the reality.

"Come on," Jake said. "I'll help you unload it."

They piled the gold and gem separator neatly, five crates and a box of parts, dreams abandoned in the dust. Jake remembered when he'd abandoned his own dreams, the day they'd buried his brother Ben outside New Orleans, eight years before.

"Catch up the teams," he ordered. "The horses are too used up to ride anymore today. We'll all walk."

The animals were redistributed to make up for those that had been killed. Cutter and the Alabamans each got an ox, as the Argonauts gave up one of their three yokes. Some of Hampton's mules went to Mrs. Skeffington and Molyneaux. With Pablo dead, Ethan took over as Mrs. Skeffington's teamster.

Lastly, there was a burial service for Pablo and Mannion and Bobby Durham. For the second time that day, the emigrants sang "Rock of Ages." Then they took their places in line, standing beside their wagons. Some sipped the remnants of precious water. Others gazed sadly behind at their belongings, at memories lost forever. Still others faced west with new confidence and determination.

At the head of the column, Jake looked them over. Whatever their official name, they were his company now. They waited for his command.

He drew a deep breath and set himself westward. "Move out!" he ordered.

9

Woodhouse shaded his eyes with his hand. "Something up ahead."

Jake looked. He saw a gray, jumbled mass, unrecognizable. "We'll find out what it is soon enough," he said with a shrug.

The two men and Dan Essex were walking. Their horses were tied to the wagon beside them. To their rear, the column of emigrants plodded along. The Cutter children and their dog were riding, peering from behind the flaps of their small wagon. Everyone else was on foot, whitened like ghosts beneath a cloud of alkali dust. There was the occasional listless snap of a bullwhip, the exhortation to some reluctant animal. The breeze had died, making the afternoon sun feel even hotter.

"You know, Jake, I envy you," Essex said. "All the opportunities you've had—Chapultapec, riding the mails, deputy sheriff. Now wagon boss. What have I done? Nothing."

Jake's spirits fell even lower than they had been. Here was handsome, assured Dan Essex, a man with real courage, with real leadership, and he looked up to a fraud like Jake. They were friends, but it was a friendship founded on lies. Jake's whole career was founded on lies. Jake wanted to tell Dan the truth about himself, but he didn't have the guts to do it.

"That's why I left the Navy," Essex went on. "I didn't mind the lack of pay, the discipline, even the bad food.

But there was no way to get ahead. Without a war, promotions are almost impossible to come by. I might still have been a lieutenant ten years from now—fifteen, even. I just feel I'm better than that.''

"You were with Perry in Japan," Woodhouse said. "Surely that was exciting."

"It would have been a lot more exciting if there had been a battle. I thought the Mexican War would prove out, but the Mexicans didn't have a navy, so we spent two years sailing around looking for something to do.'' Essex glanced sideways at Woodhouse, and his green eyes twinkled. "To be truthful, I always hoped we'd get in a war with the British. Nothing personal, Woody.''

Beneath the cocked silk hat, Woodhouse raised a thin eyebrow. "Did you, now?'' He pulled something from his dusty coat—a watch. He opened the engraved case and the watch tinkled a chorus of "Rule Britannia.''

"The lion roars,'' he said.

Jake and Essex laughed. "A gift from my mother,'' Woodhouse went on, replacing the watch. "Supposed to buck up my spirits in the wilderness, or some such nonsense. Keeps good time, though.''

"Harvey Reed thinks you're a spy for the British government,'' Jake said.

Woodhouse wrinkled both brows now and sighed. "I only wish someone had that much confidence in me. My books have been spectacularly unsuccessful. My publisher wouldn't even advance me money for this trip. I had to borrow the funds from my family. This trip will either make my career or break it.''

Essex said, "California is my big chance, too. You can't imagine how I've looked forward to this. I caught gold fever as soon as I heard about the big strike, but it took three years to get back to the U.S. When we docked at San Francisco, half the crew jumped ship and headed for the goldfields.''

"Why didn't you join them?'' Jake asked.

Essex looked a bit ruffled. "I was an officer, Jake. It was my duty to see the vessel back to port in Washington and resign honorably."

The near leader on their wagon had grown balky again. Jake jabbed the ramrod from his rifle into the ox's rump, prodding him on. Jake preferred to use the ramrod. It was hard to work the bullwhip, with its four-foot handle and twenty-foot lash.

"Will the Indians return?" Woodhouse said.

"I hope not," Jake replied. "Indians ain't got much staying power. They take what they can get—quick—then they leave. This bunch has our horses and cattle, and they've killed five of us. With any luck, that'll satisfy them."

What worried Jake more than Indians was lack of water, but he didn't say it to anyone. He might start a panic, and that was the last thing they needed. It was remarkable that the emigrants hadn't panicked already. Some of the animals were approaching the limits of their endurance, and the men were down to the last sips in their canteens.

When Jake had come across this same ground last winter, there had been water—not a lot, but enough to get them through. It had been a hot spring out here, though; most of the water had dried up. The next place they might count on water would be Comanche Crossing—a water hole so named because it sat astride one of the Indians' great war trails into Mexico. By Jake's reckoning, they were still fifty miles from Comanche Crossing—two days' travel. They had to find water before then or they were goners.

The object ahead of them was in view now. It was a pile of old lumber that at second glance resolved itself into an abandoned wagon, heavily cannibalized by passing companies for wood, canvas, and metal fittings. It lay in a heap, with the remains of the wheels nearby.

"From one of last year's parties?" Essex said.

Jake dug a grimy fingernail into the dry gray wood, picking it apart. " '52'd be my guess. Maybe even the year before."

"Hello, what's this?" said Woodhouse, farther on.

Lying on the ground was a weathered grave marker. It bore a crudely lettered inscription, much faded by the passage of time: "Our Daughter. Littel Sally. Age 4. Fever."

The bearded men fell silent. Jake turned away. He looked at the desolate horizon, breathtaking in its emptiness, burning under the fiery sun. This land lacked the spectacular beauty of the California mountains or the Mexican highlands. It lacked the Panama jungle's primitive explosion of life. It was mean and hard, and mistakes were paid for with your life. Here, survival was the only reward.

"Rider coming," Tyler Hampton said behind them.

Jake's eyes came back into focus. It was McWilliams. He reined in wearily and dismounted. He was covered with white dust. "Water ahead, 'bout two miles off."

A thin cry of relief rose from the emigrants, who had gathered around. The cry had not yet peaked when the craggy-faced Ranger added, "It's alkali, though."

"You can't drink it?" Jake said.

"I damn sure wouldn't. Couldn't get my horse to, neither."

The hopes of the thirsty emigrants deflated. Jake saw pain in some of the faces. Others hung their heads in despair.

"Well, hero, what are you going to do now?" Hampton said with an ill-humored grin.

Jake glared at him. Just then came a pistol shot from their right. Every head turned. George Lambert, the flank guard, was galloping toward the train. Behind him a huge cloud of dust was rising from folds in the earth.

"Here they come!" Lambert yelled. He was lashing the horse with his reins.

"Circle the wagons!" Jake cried.

The weary emigrants were roused to a buzz of activity. Whips cracked, parched voices were raised. Dust rose and traces jingled as the men hurried the wagons into a circle, the front wheel of one touching the rear wheel of the one before, tongues pointed inward—the way Israel Combs had taught them. Was it only this morning that Combs had been alive?

"Unhitch the animals and tie them to the wagons," Jake ordered.

Men gathered the loose stock. Others ran to their positions, taking up weapons. Lambert rode up dramatically and jumped his horse through the closing gap between two wagons. He slid from the saddle, drawing his rifle from its scabbard at the same time. Sloane was fumbling to lay out spare cartridges. Nowak, arm in a sling, propped his pistol against a wagon wheel. Mrs. Skeffington led the women in readying bandages and water.

The defenses were barely complete before the Comanches burst upon them. They thundered up in a wave, yelling.

"Don't waste ammunition!" Jake called. "Let them get close. Pick a target before you fire."

Finding the line of wagons unbroken, the Comanches swerved aside to form their own circle. Some of the emigrants opened fire.

"I said, let them get close!" Jake shouted.

The Indians circled at a distance, yelling. Suddenly they closed in. "Now!" Jake cried. The Indians fired a volley of arrows and gunshots and just as quickly moved out of range again. The emigrants fired back, but it was hard to hit moving targets, hard even to see them in the cloud of dust the circling horses created.

Again and again the Comanches moved in, now from one part of their circle, now from another. The emigrants never knew where the darting attacks would strike. They fired back, hitting nothing, frustrated. The Indians loosed off their arrows, some from beneath their horses' necks in a display of trick riding. There were cries of pain as the emigrants' animals were struck.

Some men, like Essex and McWilliams and Hampton, did well under fire. Others were shaky. Jake moved around the wagons, steadying them. He'd been in battles before, and he was as scared as ever, especially exposed like this, but it was his job. His legs trembled, and he struggled to keep his voice from breaking. "Take your time, men. Wait for a target. Willinsky, stop pointing that damn rifle up in the air—you're not shooting birds. Lambert, get under cover. Mrs. Boone, Mrs. Cutter, pass the men some water, please."

Through the swirling dust, Jake recognized Chief Patch. Red Horse was there, too. It was the same bunch that had attacked them earlier. Probably they could have overwhelmed the emigrants with one determined rush, but Comanches did not like to press home an attack. They could not afford the casualties such an attack would cause. They liked to wear you down, to grind you to death slowly.

Jake dropped to one knee beside Woodhouse. They fired and reloaded, their faces begrimed by powder and dust and sweat. Their throats were seared with thirst. An arrow thudded into the ground between them, and they traded glances.

"You can't put Comanches in a book about quadrupeds, can you?" Jake said, firing again.

The Englishman jammed another cartridge into the breech of his Sharps rifle. "Actually, I'm thinking about adding a chapter on bipeds." He aimed and fired. "Tricky getting specimens, though."

As suddenly as they had come, the Comanches withdrew. They milled in a large mass out on the plain, about a mile off. Around the wagons, there was silence. Men and women stood, watching, reloading, checking for injured.

"Anybody hurt?" Jake called.

There was no answer. "Apparently not," Dan Essex said.

"There's luck, anyway," said Woodhouse.

They waited in the heat, smelling their own sweat,

smelling the drifting powder smoke and the blood of the wounded animals. Gradually, sounds began to assert themselves—the pathetic whinny of a stricken horse, Cutter's daughter Rachel crying.

Without warning, the Indians were on them again, screaming—that awful scream that jolted along Jake's spine, that made him want to drop his rifle and run. Jesus, how did they do that? How did they move from a standing stop to a full gallop so quickly? Were they devils?

Men dove beneath the wagons again. "Steady," Jake called, trying not to sound scared. "Let them come. Harvey, open your eyes. You can't hit anything if you don't look."

Again the Comanches circled, firing as they came around the wagons. The whites fired back. There were more screams from wounded animals; the dogs were barking furiously. Jake saw Red Horse. He fired at him and missed, cursing. The Comanches lanced in so quickly that they were hard to hit. By the time you drew a bead, they were out of range again. They didn't try to break the circle of wagons; it was as if they were content with shooting the animals.

They came around in another pass. Again Jake spotted the red-painted horse through the dust. His rider came in boldly close and loosed an arrow. Beside Jake, Woodhouse fired. Red Horse reeled in his light saddle. He hung for a second by a wrist thong around his horse's neck, then his weight snapped the thong and he fell in the dust.

Red Horse rose to his feet unsteadily. Jake stepped from the protection of the wagon wheels. He drew a bead and fired. Red Horse flopped onto his back, where he kicked once and lay still.

Red Horse must have been an important war chief, for his death raised a higher-pitched, keening yell from the circling Indians. Two Comanches raced their ponies in, trying to recover his body. From beneath the next wagon, Tyler Hampton fired. One of the Comanches was jolted sideways, though he managed to stay astride his pony. He rode back to the circling braves while his companion led off Red Horse's brightly painted mount. Chief Patch waved his lance and the war party retreated, yelling, streaming back toward the horizon.

As the emigrants slowly withdrew from cover, Jake turned to Woodhouse. "Where'd you learn to shoot like that?"

Woodhouse removed his silk hat and mopped his grimy face with an even grimier handkerchief. "That's why we have country weekends. They're excellent preparation for this sort of thing."

"Comanches ain't partridges," Jake reminded him.

"Yes, they're rather larger, aren't they?"

"Will they attack again?" asked scraggly-bearded Harvey Reed.

"Maybe not," Jake said. "Indians don't populate like we do; their numbers stay about the same. It hurts them to lose any man, but especially a chief like Red Horse. A loss like that can't be made good for fifteen or twenty years."

He stopped as McWilliams climbed over the wheels between two parked wagons and ran out to the dead Indian. McWilliams drew his bowie knife and lifted Red Horse by his long hair. He locked his knees around the Indian's jaw, steadying his head. He grasped the Indian's hair with one hand, and with the other he inserted the bowie knife beneath the scalp and began sawing an incision around the top of the Indian's head.

"Oh, God," Harvey Reed said.

"Stop him," Jim Hart said, moving forward.

Jake grabbed the redhead's arm. "No, leave him be. It makes him feel better. Might be, it'll even help us."

Hart's face was filled with disgust. "How can something so vile—?"

"Indians believe if a man loses his hair after death, he don't enter the afterlife. His friends see this, it'll give 'em something to think on," Jake said.

McWilliams finished cutting. He dropped the knife and pulled with both hands, his lips drawn back in a mad grin. He pulled harder, neck muscles straining. Then he jerked back, and there was a popping sound as the scalp ripped from the dead Indian's head. Harvey Reed turned away, sick.

Hart said, "Sweet Jesus, we're just like—"

"That's right," Jake snapped, "we're just like them. This ain't James Fenimore Cooper, and that ain't Natty Bumppo. If I'd been through what McWilliams has, maybe I'd be doing the same thing right now."

McWilliams held the bloody scalp aloft, shaking it at the departed enemy, yelling savage curses. Blood had splattered his buckskins; it had splattered his face. He didn't care.

Jake went out and put a hand on the Ranger's shoulder. "Come on, son," he said quietly. He felt funny talking that way to someone older. "Let's go back."

McWilliams was breathing heavily, out of control. Spittle flecked his lips. He shoved the dripping scalp at Woodhouse. "You got him. It's yourn by rights."

The Englishman shuddered. "Not me, thanks."

"Cap'n Jake?" McWilliams said. "You finished him off."

Jake shook his head.

"I'll take it, then." McWilliams stuck the bloody scalp in his belt and moved back to the wagons, still eyeing the distant horizon. The young Argonauts moved nervously aside to let him pass. Ethan Andrews, who had been Bobby Durham's lifelong friend, did not know how to react; but George Lambert, Durham's other friend, patted McWilliams on the shoulder admiringly.

Jake looked at the dead Indian. Red Horse—or whatever his real name had been—had been young, in his early twenties. Besides his breechclout and knee-length moccasins, he wore a copper bracelet and a beaded necklace ornamented with a bear claw. The knife he had used to scalp

Bobby Durham was in a beaded sheath at his waist. Jake pulled it out. The blade had been dulled with sand, but the inscription was still legible: "R.M. DICKINSON. SHEFFIELD, ENGLAND."

Jake showed the knife to Woodhouse, who muttered, "Dreary place, Sheffield."

Jake laid the knife on the ground and snapped off the blade with his boot. He slipped Red Horse's long, feathered lance—the one with Durham's scalp—from behind the Indian's back; and, in two tries, he splintered it across his knee.

"All right," he said, raising his voice, "pick up these arrows. Break 'em in half and bury the heads—same as before. Culpepper, how are the animals?"

The tall slave limped forward, impassive as always, even though there was a new bullet hole in the crown of his glazed hat. "Two of them oxes is done for, plus a mule and one of the horses. I can save the rest that's hit, but they won't pull no weight for a couple or two days."

Jake looked over the company. After the rigors of the battle, their thirst was worse than ever. Eyes started from sockets, tongues lolled in the heat and the dust and the acrid-smelling powder smoke. "Webb, that printing press has to go. Your wagon, too. We're short of animals, and we need all our space to carry food and necessary equipment."

"Not the wagon, Captain Moran. Please, even if you take the press, don't take my—"

"It's as good as any," Jake told him. "Probably it won't be the last, neither." The bespectacled newspaperman started to plead again, but Jake cut him off. "I'm sorry, but there's no—"

"Captain?" It was Grinstead. "Take my wagon instead. I'll double up with Mr. Webb. That's if it's . . . if it's all right with him."

Webb hesitated, then nodded.

The bandaged old Yankee went on, "My wagon doesn't

mean anything to me. I'm too old to do the maintenance, and since I lost my rocking chair . . . well, all I need for California is the clothes on my back.''

Jake didn't understand Webb's fuss about his wagon, but if the problem could be settled another way, he didn't care. "Go ahead, then. Culpepper, work out the redistribution of the teams and the mending animals. Ethan, you and George help him.''

The Alabamans looked at each other. "Help him?" Ethan said. "He's a . . . a slave.''

"Just do it," Jake said. "Blade, you, Ross, and Sloane slaughter the dying animals. Cut 'em up like before. Save the blood. We'll drink it.''

The muscular Blade was sullen. "Go to hell, Moran. I ain't killin' no cows for you.''

"Me, neither," Ross said. "You been givin' me the dirty work all day.''

Jake looked at them. He'd commanded men before, but as a parade-ground officer, with the weight of the U.S. Army behind his orders. Here the only backing he had was his own moral authority. Blade and Ross were not men he would normally have tangled with, but he couldn't let them know that. "You'll do it," he said, "or you won't eat.''

Blade looked at Hampton, who seemed to be enjoying the confrontation, then he said, "So what? I'll eat pinole and bacon from the wagon.''

"No you won't. And when we get to water, you won't drink, neither." Jake jabbed his rifle barrel into Blade's thick chest, knocking him backward. "This rifle's loaded, Blade, and I'm in a mood to use it. Now get to work.''

Blade glanced at Hampton again, but the Carolinian was not ready to force the issue.

"All right," Blade said. "Come on, Jim.''

While the teams were reyoked, the wounded animals were killed and their blood collected in buckets. Each emigrant received a half cup of the liquid from ox or horse or mule, according to lot. Jake drank his in two gulps. The blood was warm and thick and salty, but it was wet. It would keep him going a little further, though the sticky aftertaste actually made him feel thirstier. Some of the emigrants, like Woodhouse and Cutter—even Mrs. Skeffington—drank without hesitation. Others, like Willinsky and Harvey Reed traded nauseous looks, then held their breaths and forced the red liquid down. The children were hesitant at first, and so were the other women, but they all drank. Molyneaux was last. "Go on," Woodhouse told him. "Pretend it's claret." Molyneaux made a face and swallowed.

"Let's get moving," Jake said.

The water hole that McWilliams had found was in a range of limestone hills to the north. The emigrants had no choice but to go there. They guided on a tall pinnacle of rock rising from the serried ridgeline. When they were within a mile, the thirsty animals became hard to control. Oxen bellowed, mules brayed, horses tugged on tethers.

"They smell the water," Jake said. "Unhitch 'em and let 'em go. We'll come back for the wagons later."

The animals trotted off across the dusty plain and up the steep hills. The emigrants followed, their hearts beating wildly despite McWilliams's negative report. They struggled up the boulder-strewn gully that led past the pinnacle and over the ridge. Jake helped Grinstead and Mrs. Boone. He offered a hand to Mrs. Skeffington, but she refused. The old woman was in better shape than he was. He wondered how she wore that whalebone corset in this suffocating heat.

Jake was the last one to pass the pinnacle and cross the ridge. The water hole, or pond, was in a shallow depression between the hills, surrounded by salt grass and a few stunted mesquite. It was a rainwater trap. The scene around it looked like something out of Noah's Ark. Oxen, horses, mules, dogs, and people were all mixed together, as if in violation of every law of Nature. The thirsty animals would put their snouts near the water, then shy back, lowing or neighing, tossing their heads or pawing the ground. Some of the humans were not so choosy. Jim Hart had plunged in his head to cool himself off. Cutter was splashing the liquid into his mouth, heedless of the danger.

Jake hurried down the hill. "Stop! Stop drinking!" He grabbed Cutter by the shoulders and dragged him away. "Stop, before you kill yourself!"

He knelt beside the pond. The surface of the water was dirty green and covered with scum. The skeleton of a longhorn cow lay nearby. The brute must have died while drinking. Jake brushed aside the scum and scooped out a handful of water. He tasted it and spit it out. "Alkali salt," he said, "and . . ." He couldn't place the other taste.

"Smells bloody awful," Woodhouse said, wrinkling his nose.

"Have the Indians poisoned it?" Essex asked.

Jake said, "Indians got too much respect for water to poison holes. Whatever it is, we sure can't drink it."

"What *do* we drink, then?" Mrs. Cutter said tearfully. Large sweat stains spread across her homespun dress. "What do the children drink?"

Everyone was looking at Jake. They were waiting for him to do something, as if he were Moses and could make fresh water burst from the rocks with a touch of his staff.

The company could go no farther, that was plain. The animals would never make it; neither would the humans. Instinct told Jake there was no other water nearby. It was drink this or die.

"Could we boil it and make tea with it?" Mrs. Skeffington wondered.

That gave Jake an idea. "Not tea. Coffee." Mrs. Skeffington didn't have enough tea for this many thirsty men and animals. Every wagon, on the other hand, carried a large supply of coffee. Coffee was the emigrants' principal drink. Even the children drank it.

Jake looked around. "Dan, you, McWilliams, and Culpepper come with me."

The four men gathered the freshest horses from around the hole, along with a team of mules. They rode back and hitched up Hampton's wagon. They ransacked the other wagons for all the coffee, coffee pots and buckets they could find, and put them in Hampton's vehicle. Then they went back to Grinstead's abandoned wagon, knocked it apart, and loaded the wood for fuel.

The afternoon was well advanced when they returned with Hampton's wagon to the water hole, whipping the team up the gully, clearing boulders from its path. The emigrants already had a fire burning from dried mesquite. "Build more fires," Jake ordered, unloading lumber. "Start filling them coffeepots. Make it strong."

The emigrants ladled filthy water from the hole and brewed coffee. It tasted horrible, but they could drink it. Pot after pot they made, and when it was ready they poured some in the buckets to cool. The rest, the thirsty people drank by the scalding cupful, even the children.

"Tell them to take it easy," Essex said to Jake. "This water can't be good for us."

"What use would it be?" Jake said. "They won't stop. This might be the only water for fifty miles; and if it is, they'll need all of it they can get."

When the buckets were cooled, the emigrants led the animals to them in relays. The beasts balked at first, fighting their handlers, especially the oxen and Molyneaux's $4,000 thoroughbred, who tried to bite Culpepper.

Molyneaux slapped the slave alongside the ear. "Be careful with that horse, damn you. He cost twice as much as you did."

Culpepper said nothing. It was not the first time he'd been struck on this trip.

Extreme thirst finally drove the animals to sample the rancid coffee. They tasted, snorted, then went back for more.

"They're drinking!" cried Cutter. "Thank the Lord!"

"Jake, you're a genius!" laughed Molyneaux.

"Good ole Jake," George Lambert said.

"It was Mrs. Skeffington's idea, not mine," Jake said, but no one was paying attention. "Keep that coffee coming! It'll take all evening to water these animals, and we'll want more for the morning."

Jake tried not to think about that longhorn skeleton and that strange taste he'd noticed in the water. He tried not to think about the possible consequences of drinking it. For the moment, the company was saved, and the moment was all that mattered. They would face the future as it came.

10

"Now what?" asked Tyler Hampton.

"What do you mean?" said Jake.

The setting sun had turned the sky reddish orange. The pinnacle of rock rose from the ridgeline above them, glowing gold in the last rays of daylight. In the gathering shadows below the pinnacle, the oxen wandered the rock-strewn hillside, grazing on the sparse grass and shrubbery, lying down for the night. Hidden in the rocks, George Lambert was posted as a sentry. Frank Sloane stood guard on the other side of the camp.

Hampton went on, waving a fat cigar he had lit from the fire, "I mean, do we stay here or go on? There's a lot to be said for sitting tight. There's water here and grass for the animals. The area is easy to defend."

"Why stay?" Jake said.

The dark-browed Carolinian looked at him with the contempt reserved for stupidity. "To wait for the Comanches to go away. To wait for them to get tired of attacking us and go wherever the hell they were headed before we ran into them."

There were murmurs of assent from around the fires. The emigrants were tired and scared. Their eyes were sunken. Even Mrs. Skeffington was unusually subdued. Some of them watered the last of the horses with the cold coffee, then led the animals off to be picketed for the night near the mules. Others scraped the remains of cornmeal mush from frying pans or gnawed steaks charred over mesquite fires.

"I don't like it," Jake told him. "Like Dan said, this water might be killing us; we don't want to drink too much of it. With the cattle herd gone, we're short of food, too. We can't keep eating our draft animals."

"Hampton's not saying we should spend the rest of our lives here," Webb said, cleaning his eyeglasses with a handkerchief. "Just a few days. What about the Comanches?"

"I'm guessin' they're gone," Jake said.

"And what if they ain't?" asked Blade.

"If they ain't, they know where we are. We can fort up here, sure, but they'll have a field day picking off our animals. And even if we live through that, and this coffee-water don't run out, we'll be looking at a long walk to El Paso, and walking means we can't carry much food nor spare water. I don't see we got a choice, 'cept keep moving."

Hampton swore with disgust. There was some muttering and shifting of seats, but most of the emigrants agreed with Jake. Many of them trusted him blindly, even those—like Essex—who should have known better.

The light was almost gone now. The pinnacle of rock stood black against the orange sky, like a warning, or a giant totem left from another age. The prairie was silent. The daytime creatures had gone; the night life had yet to emerge. The smells of fires and coffee and burned steaks mingled with those of pipe tobacco and Hampton's cigar.

"Least the full moon is past," McWilliams said, squatting on his heels. The craggy-faced Ranger was drinking the last of his coffee. "If it was full tonight, we could expect the Comanch' to come with it. That's when they like to fight."

"And now?" Jake said.

McWilliams shrugged. "Mebbe they had enough, like you say."

Something droned in Jake's ear, and he slapped his

cheek, "Mosquitoes! Just what we need." He stood. "Let's douse these fires. Whether the Indians is gone or not, there's no need to make ourselves good targets. Keep one lit for making more coffee."

The rest of the wagons had been brought up and circled. Everyone settled in as best they could, wrapping blankets around themselves, sleeping in the wagon beds or lying back to back on the cold earth. Jake heard Mrs. Skeffington leading the Cutter children in their prayers.

Jake remembered other evenings in camp. After supper, Cutter would pull out his fiddle and play "Turkey in the Straw," "Oh, California!" or one of a dozen other tunes. Maybe there would be dancing, the men asking Mrs. Boone or Mrs. Cutter by turns—no one dared ask Mrs. Skeffington. Sometimes the men danced with each other, the designated "lady" tying a handkerchief around his left arm. When Cutter was done, Nowak would produce his violin and entertain them with European waltzes and polkas. Afterward, there might be singing, sentimental songs to remind them of home. Or there would be a game of poker, Jake playing—on borrowed money—with Molyneaux, Essex, Hampton, and Israel Combs, with maybe Jim Hart or Webb joining in. Woodhouse would be sitting by the fire, sketching or examining some new specimen. Mrs. Skeffington would be admonishing the men for their profanity or complaining that the ladies' latrines were too shallow. Over all would be the sound of the children—laughing, chasing each other around the wagons, playing with their dog. Now there were only restless turnings and snores, the low crackle of the fire, the shuffle of an animal.

The stars were still faint. Jake opened Woodhouse's watch, which he had borrowed earlier, shaking his head as the watch tinkled "Rule Britannia." It was time to change sentries. Wearily, he took the dark-lantern from Hampton's wagon and prodded two recumbent figures with his boot. "Willinsky, Ross. Guard."

The men took their weapons. Grumbling, the gold-toothed killer Ross started up the ridge to relieve Sloane. Jake walked with Willinsky. The young New Yorker had stood guard before, but never on a night like this. "Jesus, Jake. Jesus, I'm scared," he said as Jake led him up the hillside, using the lantern's beam to guide them. Willinsky's face was drawn; he held his rifle awkwardly. His clothes hung on his once-fat frame, his striped pants were torn, and his odd-looking, nearly brimless hat was crushed in the crown.

"Don't worry," Jake told him. "Prob'ly them Comanches is long gone, for Mexico or the Llano Estacado. You just stay awake and keep your eyes peeled, and you'll be all right."

The position Jake had picked was in a crevice between two fallen boulders that had long ago been part of the pinnacle. From here there was a good view of both the prairie and the camp, and it would be hard to surprise someone inside.

"See anything?" Jake whispered to Lambert as they came up.

The blond Alabaman shook his head. "Not a thing." He started down the hill, tired and anxious to turn in.

With the lantern, Jake showed Willinsky the sentry position. The Jewish boy settled his ample frame between the sharp rocks, shifting until he found a comfortable position. He tried to look brave, but his lower lip was trembling. It was bad enough being with your comrades in hostile territory, but it was scary as hell out here alone in the blackness of the night.

"Challenge before you fire," Jake told him. "It could be one of us. We'll relieve you in two hours."

Willinsky nodded. Jake patted his shoulder. "You'll be all right." Willinsky nodded again, and Jake started back down the hill.

This was a good time for Willinsky to pull guard. Jake wanted his best men on duty right before dawn. That was the likely time for an attack, if there was to be one. The frightened look on Willinsky's face brought back memories. Jake had looked that way himself once, on guard duty in Mexico, when the *guerrilleros* were slitting the throats of American sentries, or dragging them off to be tortured. Probably he would look that way now, if people weren't always watching him.

He returned to the fire and sat wearily. He would stay awake to relieve the guards, then turn the duty over to Essex. Culpepper was the only one still up, tending the coffee.

For a long time Jake gazed into the flames, smoking *cigaritos*, swatting the mosquitoes that buzzed around him, and trying not to fall asleep. His body ached. He would have given anything for a bottle of whiskey, for the mindless oblivion that whiskey could bring. All around were the noises of sleeping men and women. Across from him, Culpepper said not a word. The black man poured the coffee into the buckets with that impassive look, as if Jake were not even there. He made Jake feel uncomfortable. That wasn't right. Culpepper was the slave; if anyone should be uncomfortable, it was him.

"Mind if I ask you a question?" Jake said.

Culpepper grunted. "What I mind don't make no difference."

"How come you never run away?"

The black man laughed to himself. "Oh, I run away. More'n oncet."

"What happened?"

"You really want to know?"

Jake was disconcerted by Culpepper's tone. "Yeah."

"Well, the first time, Mistuh Langdon he caught me and he chained my leg across a log. Then he pulled out my toenails, one by one, with pliers." The slave watched Jake's reaction, then he went on, "And the second time . . ."

He rolled up his plaid trousers and held his right leg close to the firelight. The leg was marked with deep gouges and scars, where chunks of flesh had been ripped away. Jake flinched.

"The second time he set the dogs on me. They's his nigger-catchin' dogs. That's why he brung 'em, to keep me from runnin' ag'in. Won't be no third time, though. I don't want no more parts of them dogs."

"You could have stole a horse anytime since we left San Antone," Jake said. "You could have outrode them dogs and gone to Mexico. You still could."

"I thought 'bout it. I thought 'bout stealin' *his* horse. But he'd jest come after me. Don't matter how so much a start I'd got, nor how many Indians was between us. He'd foller me into Mexico; he'd foller me into Hell. That's the way he was raised up to do."

"You resigned to bein' a slave, then?" Jake said.

"I'm resigned to waitin' on my chance. Maybe I can get freed in Arizona somehow." He laughed bitterly. "Maybe the U.S. of A. Government will say they cain't be no slaves no more." He stirred the fire, put on more coffee. "Anyways, Mistuh Langdon he ain't so bad, as white folks go. Could be I belonged to Mistuh Hampton, with that fella Blade as overseer. Now, what you think that would be like?"

Jake didn't think it would be too good. "You don't like white people much, do you?"

Culpepper shot him a withering look.

"No," Jake said. "Well, I reckon I don't blame you."

Nearby, Cutter's gray terrier Sparky, who had been dragging a bone around, chewing on it, began growling in a low voice. He growled louder, hunched protectively over his bone. His ears were up. Some of the horses grew uneasy, tugging their picket lines.

There was another, deeper growl, then suddenly the little dog was on his feet, baying wildly, in a strident tone that made Jake jump. The dog ran to the edge of Hampton's wagon, then back again, barking for all he was worth.

The horses began stamping and neighing. The mules

brayed. Molyneaux's mastiffs, chained to a mesquite bush, woke and took up the cry. Men—Essex, McWilliams—tumbled sleepily to their feet, grabbing weapons. "What the—!"

Hampton was up, too. "Goddamn that dog!" Sparky had done this four or five times every night since they had left San Antonio. "Cutter, if you don't shoot that cur, I will!"

The barking dog was pointed toward the rock pinnacle, unseen now in the blackness. The camp was in an uproar, men and animals. "What's going on? Somebody shut that damn fool dog up!"

There was a shout from the direction of Ross's guard position, then a flash of light and a rifle shot.

"Stand to arms!" Jake ordered.

Cursing, men snatched their weapons and moved to their assigned positions. There were no more shots.

Jake cupped his hand and called, "Ross!"

"Somethin' out there!" came the Missourian's voice from the rocks. "It's gone now."

Sparky had not stopped barking. He would continue like this for a half hour sometimes before he gave up. "Willinsky!" Jake called above the racket. "You hear anything?"

There was no answer. Just the barking.

Cutter aimed a kick at Sparky's ribs. "Shut up, will you!" The terrier yelped and ran under Hampton's wagon, where he defiantly kept up a half growl, half bark.

"Willinsky!" Jake yelled again. "Willinsky! Damn it, answer!"

Still no sound but the dogs and the horses and the hoofbeats of disturbed oxen on the hillside.

"Willinsky!"

Somebody had to go up there. Jake swore, because he knew that somebody had to be him. He looked around. "I'll come with you," Essex said.

"No, I want you here, to take command in case something happens to me."

"Hell, I'll go with you," Culpepper said.

"Me, too," said Willinsky's college friend, Jim Hart.

Jake took the dark-lantern. The three men drew revolvers. They advanced past the fire, past Hampton's wagon and into the inky darkness. They picked their way slowly among the rocks and brush and jumbled boulders of the hillside. Above them, the pinnacle was felt rather than seen, a looming mass in the greater blackness around them. Despite his limp, Culpepper kept up with the other two.

Jake heard something moving, to their right. He tapped the shoulders of the others. They pointed their revolvers, cocking them. The sound came closer. Jake felt the hair rising on the back of his neck. His finger was curling on the trigger, when the object lowed plaintively. It was one of their oxen.

The three men let out their breaths. They lowered the hammers of their revolvers and kept moving. Hart slipped on some rocks and slid a few feet down the hill. Jake stubbed a toe painfully and bit back an oath. Anyone could have heard them a mile away. Why hadn't Willinsky challenged?

"Steve!" hissed Jim Hart, calling Willinsky by his first name.

Nothing. Below them, the commotion had died, though Sparky still barked fitfully. Jake was trembling, cold inside. He had a terrible foreboding. He pulled the slide on the dark-lantern and shone the light around the hill. They were slightly down and to the left of the sentry position. They fixed the position in the lantern beam and moved forward.

Jake shone the lantern inside the rocks. Willinsky lay sprawled against the far corner. There was an arrow in his chest. The arrow had gone almost clean through him; the feathers were buried in his body. The protruding shaft had been broken by his fall. On the balding young Argonaut's face was a look of shock.

Hart fell to a knee beside his dead friend. He hung his head. "Oh, no," he said.

Jake swore silently to himself. "Poor kid."

"Must have been they come awful close, to put an arrow through him like that," Culpepper said.

"Maybe he fell asleep," Jake said. "Maybe he just didn't hear them coming."

"Got his rifle and pistol, too. Didn't scalp him, though."

"Cutter's dog scared 'em off, like as not. Even with that little bit of hair, they'd have scalped him otherwise," Jake said. He let out his breath. "No sense lookin' for the cattle in the dark. If the Comanches ain't killed them, they ain't strayed far. They're too tired. Come on, let's get this body down the hill. Culpepper, stay here on guard."

By the lantern's light, Culpepper found a new sentry position in the rocks. "Be careful," Jake told him, unnecessarily. Then Jake and Jim Hart lifted Willinsky's body and made their way slowly back to the water hole. The body was heavy, and the two men stumbled on the rocks and the steep hill.

Jake felt empty inside, angry as well. He blamed himself for Willinsky's death. He should never have let somebody that inexperienced stand guard. But every man had to take his turn, that was how you got experience. You couldn't just have the same three or four people awake all night. Still, there must have been something he could have done differently, something that would have kept the boy alive. A better position? Those rocks were a natural fort. The only way the Indians could have found Willinsky was if he had been making noise, or . . . or if they had seen the guards taking position while it was still light.

A shiver rippled up Jake's spine. Had the emigrants been watched the whole time they had been at the water hole?

One thing was clear—the Comanches were still around. And Jake did not now think it likely that they would go away.

11

Jake stood the company to arms well before dawn, anticipating an attack. While half the men stood guard, the fires were relit. More coffee was brewed, and the long process of watering the stock began. Horses were grained and saddled. Mules were hitched to their wagons. Canteens and water casks were filled.

"This muck doesn't taste any better than it did yesterday," said Woodhouse from his position beneath the rock pinnacle. He shivered in the pre-dawn chill and swirled his coffee in a tin cup.

"This is nothing," Dan Essex said, grinning at the Englishman's pained expression. "When I was junior midshipman on the old *Ohio*, and you got coffee at night, you had to clench your teeth when you drank it to keep the cockroaches in the bottom of the mug from going into your mouth."

"How wonderful," murmured Woodhouse.

Gray light spread slowly across the prairie, revealing no sign of the Comanches. "Where have they gone?" said red-haired Jim Hart, further down the ridge.

Beside him, Jake shook his head, scratching vigorously at a mosquito bite on his hand. "I've given up trying to figure them bastards out. I thought sure they'd come with first light."

The oxen were rounded up. One was found with two arrows in its back. Another stood pitifully, hamstrung on all four legs by a Comanche knife. "Stop staring," Jake told the men who had gathered around the stricken animals. "You know what to do with them oxes. Cut 'em up quick and cook 'em. We'll eat the steaks on the trail." Then he added, "This means we have to leave another wagon."

He looked toward the giant Conestoga of the New York Gold Hunters Association. "Ours?" the ex-orchestra leader Nowak said.

Jake saw the Argonauts' saddened faces. "I'm sorry. I know it cost you a lot of money, but it's the heaviest, the hardest on the animals. You boys will have to split your supplies among the rest." He raised his voice, addressing the company. "We got a hard pull ahead of us. We have to lighten these wagons again. If it ain't food nor ammunition, get rid of it."

He paused. "No complaints, Mr. Webb?"

The newspaperman licked his lips. "No complaints."

There was another unloading of goods—tin pans for washing gold, cookware, daguerreotypes, bundles of folded letters, and mementos of former lives. At the last moment, Harvey Reed retrieved the "EXCELSIOR" flag from the abandoned Conestoga. He folded it and stuffed it in his shirt.

"Even if we get to California, we won't be able to mine any gold," Essex said, tossing his pick and shovel on the growing pile of equipment.

"We'll be dumping food next," Jake told him. "We was supposed to have food enough to get us to California. Now I ain't even sure we'll make El Paso."

When the oxen were yoked, the emigrants buried Willinsky. Jim Hart read from the Book of Psalms. Willinsky's death greatly affected the three remaining New Yorkers. They had planned this trip for more than two years, saving money, waiting for Hart and Willinsky to finish college. It was to have been the adventure of a lifetime. Never had they imagined such tragedy.

When the burial was over, the line of wagons rolled across Willinsky's grave. The sun was just rising as they pulled out of the hills and onto the plain, leaving behind the red-white-and-blue Conestoga with its proud lettering, a monument to the price paid for moving west.

Quickly it grew hot. There was no shade, no prospect of water. They could not reach Comanche Crossing before tomorrow evening at the earliest. Watching the wagons file by, Jake wondered how many of these tired animals would make it. He wondered how many of the people would make it, and he wished like hell that getting them through was someone else's responsibility.

At mid-morning, the sky ahead filled with buzzards. There were dozens of them, circling, flapping to the ground. The emigrants traded anxious glances. Soon they were assailed by an overwhelming stench. The animals balked at going closer. The buzzards could be seen feeding on dark masses scattered across the plain.

"Buffalo?" Essex asked.

"I don't think so," Jake said. Halting the train, he and the ex-sailor drew their bandanas over their faces and rode forward.

They found the ground littered with dead cattle, round-bellied Eastern stock and Spanish longhorns mixed together. The buzzards gorged themselves on the stiffened carcasses, hardly bestirring themselves at the approach of the horsemen. The stench was so powerful that it was almost impossible to breathe. Huge black-and-green bottle flies got in Jake's eyes; they swarmed under his bandana, in his mouth. The air vibrated with their buzzing. The horses shied and tried to run away.

The cattle had had their throats slit. Coagulated blood lay in thick black pools. Swollen stomachs had been ripped open, and rotting viscera trailed across the ground where wolves and coyotes had dragged them.

"It's our cattle herd," Jake told the emigrants, when he and Essex returned to the wagons.

"My God," breathed Langdon Molyneaux.

Cutter, who had brought many of the cattle to stock a

farm in California, sagged noticeably. His wife, Melissa, held on to his arm, giving strength to him and to herself. "That . . . that's inhuman," she said. "Such a waste. Why did they do it? Why?"

"It ain't a waste to them," Jake said. "Comanches eat buffalo. They get near everything they need from buffalo. It's beneath them to have truck with cattle, 'less they're starving. They left this in our path to show their contempt for us."

The wagons detoured around the dead cattle. As they did, McWilliams and Jim Hart, who had been detailed as hunters, rode in. A look at their empty saddles told that they had not found game.

"Comanche sign everywhere," McWilliams said. "We're heading right into them."

Jake sighed. What choice did they have?

Soon the inevitable dust was sighted. "Circle the wagons," Jake ordered.

This time the Comanches did not burst upon the wagon train. They made a leisurely approach, while the emigrants waited nervously, sighting down their rifles. When the Indians were within a half mile, Chief Patch led them into a yelling circle. They made one attack, loosing a volley of arrows. Then they retreated while the whites fired after them.

"Gutless sonsabitches," swore George Lambert. "They seen enough of these circled wagons, that's what it is. They don't want no more parts of us."

The emigrants waited, sweating under the hot sun, gagging on the stench of the slaughtered cattle. Mrs. Boone fainted and had to be revived with precious coffee-water. The Comanches did not renew the attack. At last Jake gave the order, and the whites began the laborious task of re-hitching the teams, forming up, and moving on.

They had barely started to move when Jake cried, "They're coming again! Circle! Circle!"

Again the forted-up emigrants awaited the onslaught of

the Indians. Again Chief Patch led his painted warriors in a yelling ride around the wagons. The whites fired some long shots and succeeded only in wasting powder and downing an Indian's pony. The Comanches charged in twice, halfheartedly it seemed, shooting their arrows and firearms from a greater range than before, doing nothing beyond placing an arrow in a mule's rump. Then they retreated again, to the jeers and catcalls of the increasingly confident whites.

Once more, the emigrants hitched their teams. Jake was expecting another attack, and before the company had gone a mile it came. Jake did not have to order the wagons circled, the men did it automatically.

The wagons were moved into their defensive positions more slowly this time. The men were tired and thirsty from their exertions. Some sneaked drinks from their canteens, though Jake had warned them to conserve. This time the Comanches did not attack at all. They sat their horses in a mass a mile off, watching. Jake made out the powerful form of Patch at their front.

The standoff continued for nearly an hour. Then Patch signaled with his lance and the Indians rode away once more.

"Cowards!" yelled Ross after them.

"Come back and fight!" cried Cutter, still seething at the callous slaughter of his cattle.

Other men laughed or shook hands, convinced they had taken the measure of the enemy, convinced the worst was over. "They're scared to take us on again, aren't they, Jake?" Sloane said, revealing a gap where a tooth had been knocked out in his fight with Mannion.

"No, they ain't scared," Jake said. He was scowling, and his scowl grew darker by the second, because he knew what Patch was up to. "They aim to wear us out. They aim to keep us circled up and away from water. They're doing a good job of it, too. We ain't come three miles since we broke camp. We won't make ten for the day, at this rate. They'll keep us circling these wagons till we're worn out and dropping over with thirst, and then they'll ride in and kill us without a fight.''

Jake kicked the ground, as much in frustration with himself as in anger at the Indians. ''I can't figure it. It ain't like Indians to stick with something this way. It's that chief of theirs, the one with the mourning patch shaved out of his hair. He's outthought us and outfought us. He's made fools of us. Who the hell is he?''

''I know who he is,'' said someone. It was Mrs. Skeffington.

Jake turned, eyes wide with surprise. Mrs. Skeffington was staring at the horizon, where the Indians had disappeared. Beneath her sunbonnet, her gray hair was now frazzled. She had lost weight, and the loss made her sharp nose look more pointed than ever. Her voice was unusually soft. ''I've seen him before. I've been introduced to him, if you can believe that. His name is Yellow Wolf. He's the great war chief of the Nokoni Comanches. Last year, his only son, Swift Cloud, was invited to a peace parley outside San Antonio. Swift Cloud was one of the most feared raiders on the Texas frontier. Soon after the 'parley' started, Swift Cloud was arrested, shot, and killed. 'Trying to escape,' the report said. But it was really murder.''

''How do you know all this?'' Jake said.

''My . . . my husband was a member of the 'peace' commission. He tried to stop the Militia from killing the boy. Israel Combs was there, too, with the Militia.''

''So that's it,'' said Jake. ''This is a revenge war. Patch—Yellow Wolf—didn't kill enough in the settlements to make up for the loss of his son. He wants our scalps, too. We're all Tejanos to him—blood enemies. His medicine must be mighty strong to hold so many warriors together this long.''

''Mebbe it's got somethin' to do with Combs bein' killed,'' said the Ranger McWilliams. ''Them Indians all knowed who Combs was. They must know they got him.

That's big medicine for any chief, even if they missed get-tin' his scalp.''

"Which leaves us the question of what to do next," Woodhouse said.

"Think fast, hero," Tyler Hampton said. Hampton actually looked happy at Jake's predicament.

Jake ignored the Carolinian. "We got no choice. We'll never make Comanche Crossing this way. From now on, there'll be no more circling the wagons. We'll have to fight our way through."

"Oh, this is rich," swore Hampton, "All we've been hearing from you is 'circle the wagons, we have to circle the wagons.' That's been your answer to everything. But now the great Jake Moran changes his mind. We don't want to circle the wagons, he says. No, we want to fight our way through. Face it, Moran, you don't know what the hell you're talking about."

"Shut up, you idiot," Jake said. He'd had enough of Hampton's second guesses, and he was irritated because he thought there was a lot of truth in what Hampton had said. "If you were still in charge, we wouldn't have made it this far. I should have shot you when I was of a mind."

Hampton bristled. His round face went red, and he took a step forward, as if to hit Jake. Then he stopped and grinned. Jake knew Hampton's game; he'd seen his kind before. Hampton would try to undermine Jake's authority, then make his move when he had the majority of the emigrants behind him.

Jake strove to control his anger. If the Indians had to kill somebody, why hadn't they killed Hampton? "All right," he said, addressing the company, "we'll noon here. Grab something to eat, and have some water—but not too much. After this, there'll be no stopping till we make camp."

The emigrants shifted uneasily as Jake explained what he intended. They were covered with dust; the men's beards were white with it. There were dark bags under their eyes. Their clothes were torn. They reeked of stale sweat.

"What happens if the Indians attack?" asked old Grinstead, who had jammed his hat over his bandaged head.

"We keep walking," Jake told him. "We walk through whatever they throw at us."

12

A scant hour later, with the sun just past its zenith and the hottest part of the day ahead, the company started off. There were eight wagons, the four drawn by mules leading, the four drawn by oxen coming behind. The leaders of each wagon were right on the tailboard of the wagon in front. The horses were tied to the wagons. The teamsters rode or walked the near side, cracking their whips; nine men—and women—walked the off side. They were armed with Sharps rifles, with Hawkens, even Cutter's old .44 Kentucky flint-lock. Jake and Hampton walked the point; Essex and Woodhouse brought up the rear.

"There they are!" yelled Ross, teamster on Hampton's number-two wagon.

To the left rose a plume of dust as the Comanches advanced in a long file, on a course that would take them in front of the wagons.

Jake tried not to tremble, especially with Hampton next to him, watching. He prayed the Indians wouldn't attack, but he knew there was no chance of that. They were closing. He had no idea if his plan would work. It had to work. If it didn't, the emigrants would die.

"Don't stop, no matter what," he called over his shoulder. "Fire as you go, don't worry about ammunition. Make them keep their distance."

The Comanches broke into a trot, yelling, riding across the front of the emigrant column, beginning their circle. This is it, Jake thought. He raised his Sharps and opened the ball. His first shot knocked a howling Indian from his horse.

Hampton looked over at Jake. "Nice shooting," he said begrudgingly. That had not been the Indian at whom Jake was aiming, but Jake wasn't going to tell Hampton that.

There was a ragged cheer from the column. "Way to go, Captain Jake!" whooped Harvey Reed.

"We should send you out there by yourself, Jake," laughed George Lambert, "just like before. Them kind of odds don't bother you none."

Jake's lucky shot made the Indians keep a respectful distance—at first. They formed a moving circle around the column. There were at least a hundred of them. The emigrants didn't wait for them to close, they fired as they walked along. They kept a steady pace, firing and reloading. Acrid powder smoke and dust drifted down. They heard the Indians yelling. They heard the tinkling of the little bells that the Indians braided into their horses' manes. From time to time groups of Indians dashed in. Bullets zipped by; arrows whistled. It was hardest on the teamsters. The muleskinners had to fire from the saddle and manage their animals at the same time. The bullwhackers cracked their long, cumbersome whips, then shifted the whips to fire their weapons. As they passed the Indian that Jake had shot, McWilliams ran out and scalped him, but no one paid attention this time.

Jake hated being out front, but it was part of being in command; there was no way to avoid it. Beside him, Hampton marched along, picking his targets, firing his Sharps rifle. Hampton had guts, Jake had to give him that. An arrow hit the ground at Jake's feet, and he stumbled over it.

There was Yellow Wolf, riding boldly, exhorting his warriors. Jake wondered if Yellow Wolf recognized him; he wondered if Yellow Wolf remembered the white leader as the man he'd let live yesterday. Yellow Wolf was the key; he was the one who held the Indians together. Kill him, and this nightmare might end. The next time Yellow Wolf raced by, Jake drew a bead on him. As he squeezed the trigger, he remembered the old Indian's fathomless brown eyes and his majestic presence, and he almost hoped that he missed. For a moment, dust obscured the results of his shot. Then he saw that Yellow Wolf was down, along with his horse. The Indian chief leapt to his feet, however, and was pulled up behind a following brave, who carried him from the circle for a new mount. Yellow Wolf's horse thrashed on the ground, the front of its head blown away by the .50-caliber Sharps bullet.

Jake lost track of time in the heat and the dust and the din of gunfire. Again and again the yelling Indians charged the column, aiming for the center, trying to break the formation. Again and again, fire by whites drove them back. The Indians could crush the whites by sheer numbers if they wished, but Jake counted on that reluctance to force home an attack and take heavy casualties.

"Keep 'em moving," Jake told Hampton. He untied his horse from Hampton's wagon and rode down the line. "Keep going!" he yelled hoarsely. "Stay closed up, there. Keep moving." He saw Mrs. Skeffington. The old woman marched along like a seasoned campaigner, firing and reloading unhurriedly. Her gray hair had come unpinned; her face was streaked with sweat and black powder smoke.

There was a gap between Webb's wagon and Molyneaux's in front of it. "Keep this thing moving," Jake yelled at Webb and his teamster, Nowak.

The fiercely mustachioed Nowak had stripped the sling from his arm and put down his rifle. He whirled his long bullwhip over his head and cracked it repeatedly. "The wheels have shrunk away from the tires in this heat," he shouted to Jake. "It makes her to wobble."

"Webb, you ain't hiding anything in there, are you?" Jake said. "Anything that makes this wagon heavy?"

"No," said Webb, whose glasses were begrimed with dust. "Look for yourself. It's the wheels."

As Webb spoke, one of Molyneaux's mules went down. "Cut it out of the traces," Jake yelled at Culpepper. He dismounted to help, but Culpepper was already in action with his knife. Jake fired his rifle, covering the sweating slave. Molyneaux's wagon got moving again, and Jake waved Webb after it. "Go, go!"

He remounted his horse and continued down the line. No one was panicking. Mrs. Cutter and her widowed sister, Mrs. Boone, walked together. They were pioneer women, and they knew how to use firearms—even if Mrs. Boone was shooting high. The Cutter girl, Rachel, was under cover in the wagon, with the dog, Sparky, while nine-year-old Richard was bravely carrying cartridges and percussion caps from the wagons to the men on the line.

Jake reached the rear of the column. Essex and Woodhouse were walking slowly, turning and firing at the screaming Comanches, keeping them at a distance. Jake wheeled his horse and fell in beside them. A bullet holed his sleeve, but he pretended not to notice. "Everything all right?" he said.

"Simply ripping," Woodhouse said. "Our Ancient Mariner here actually enjoys this sort of thing."

Essex grinned at him. "Come on, Woody, you wanted some adventure on this trip, didn't you?"

"My idea of adventure is finding that my cellar is down to its last bottle of port."

Jake unscrewed his canteen top and slaked his thirst with the warm, brackish coffee-water. The liquid tasted horrible and wonderful at the same time. Jake drank in small swallows, so no drops would be lost.

Woodhouse fired at the circling Indians. "Tell me," he shouted, "where do the Indians get their water? Or do they just not need the stuff?"

"They need it," Jake said, replacing his canteen on his Texas-rigged saddle. "But a Comanche can take more hardship than we can, and so can his horse. I heard of 'em riding a hundred miles without a stop. Probably they're operating in relays, riding to a spring in the mountains, bringing back water in tied-up buffalo guts. They bring extra horses to war, so they've got plenty of fresh remounts.''

Jake rode back to the front of the column. He tied his horse to the wagon once more and rejoined Hampton. The column was making decent progress, though they were using a prodigious amount of ammunition. That couldn't be helped. Having ammunition would make no difference if they didn't reach water. The crash of gunfire, the yells of Indians made it almost impossible to think. Hampton was pointing at something. There was a ravine in their path. Jake saw dismounted Indians filtering into it.

''Blade! Hart!'' Jake waved the first two riflemen from the wagons forward. ''We'll skirmish our way through. Clear that ravine.''

The four men walked in line in front of the oncoming wagons. Puffs of smoke came from the ravine, though they couldn't hear the shots over the general din. Jake and his men opened fire, moving forward all the time, pausing only to lever open their rifle breeches and jam in more cartridges.

They neared the ravine, firing into the brush that lined its edge. Suddenly the Indians broke cover and ran for their horses. Jake fired his rifle at them. He transferred the rifle to his left hand, drawing his back revolver. He yelled with pain and dropped the rifle as the red-hot barrel seared his hand. While Jake shook his burned hand, swearing, the other skirmishers fired after the retreating Indians. One of the braves pitched forward onto his face. Another grabbed his leg and hobbled to his mount, got on, and rode away.

As Hampton passed in pursuit of the fleeing Indians, another Indian rose from the brush behind him, bow drawn. Jake snapped a revolver shot at the brave, spinning him back into the brush.

Hampton turned at the sound of the shot. He looked at

Jake, grinning. "Thanks, Moran. Don't expect me to do the same for you, though."

"I won't," Jake said. For a second, he wondered if he should have saved Hampton, but he'd had no choice. He couldn't have stood by and watched him be shot in the back.

The four skirmishers scoured the ravine, but they found no more Indians. The brave Jake had downed was only wounded. Blade stood over him and shot him in the head.

Hampton's number-one wagon approached the ravine, which was shallow but steep. The men found a slight incline to work the wagons down. There were no brakes on the wagons; there was no time to rough-lock the wheels with chains, or to attach long ropes to ease the wagons down the drop. They had to take their chances. The mules went over, sliding on the incline, with their teamster, Mc-Williams, holding them in. Then came the wagon, bouncing down in a cloud of dust, in a clatter of fittings and equipment and groaning wood. The wagon crossed the ravine and started up the other side, with McWilliams yelling and whipping the team on.

The next wagon started over the edge. Driven inexpertly by Ross, the mules slipped. The wagon bounced off a large rock near the top, skewed crazily to its side, and dropped down, crashing hard on the rocky bottom, where it lay with its front wheels tilted up, the axle broken clean.

"Drag it out of the way!" shouted Jake. "Make room for the others!" He grabbed the mules' harness and began pulling the broken wagon to one side. Hart flung his weight on the mules' other side to help him. "Cut the mules loose and leave the wagon," Jake went on. "There's no time to fix it." He moved forward, waving the next wagon—Mrs. Skeffington's—over the lip of the ravine. His burned hand hurt like hell.

"What about the food inside?" Ross asked, dismounting the near wheeler of his team.

"No room to carry it in the other wagons," Jake told

him over the noise of shouting teamsters, over the gunfire
and the braying mules. "Take out the powder and cartridges and stow them in the next wagon."

One by one, the wagons dropped down the side of the
rocky ravine. They passed the abandoned wagon and
climbed the far side while sweating, cursing men whipped
the mules and oxen as they heaved on the wheels. A sudden charge of Indians straight down the ravine was met by
a hail of rifle and pistol shots. The Indians fired and retreated.

Across the ravine, the wagons formed up and kept moving. Jake mounted his horse. He rode up and down the
line, urging the tired emigrants on. He lost count of the
number of times the screaming savages charged; he lost
count of the times he fired at them. He wondered if this
day would ever end. If it did end, he wondered if they
could live through another day like it. It seemed there was
never a time he hadn't heard the yelling of Indians, the
bang of rifles and pop of revolvers.

The Indians circled closer and closer. Yellow Wolf was
back at their head, riding a pure white horse. The Indians
were no longer galloping; they moved at a fast walk. They
were nearly as exhausted as the whites. The rate of defensive fire slackened. The whites could not hold back the red
tide much longer. With the shortened range, men and animals were more vulnerable. Another mule went down. It
was cut out and one of Hampton's hurried into its place.
A wounded ox was dragged from its yoke.

The sun was westering, but darkness would not come
soon enough to save the emigrants. Jake thought that Yellow Wolf would wait till exactly sunset, then make a sudden rush to try to end it. By then, the exhausted whites
would be in no shape to offer much resistance.

The off leader on Hampton's remaining wagon took an
arrow in the eye. It began to buck wildly, pulling its wagon
to one side. While McWilliams and Blade tried to steady
the rest of the team, Hart alertly put a revolver bullet in

the mule's head, dropping it in its tracks. Then a chance shot parted the line tying Molyneaux's $4,000 thorough-bred to his wagon. The high-strung horse began to move away from the column. It passed Mrs. Skeffington, who instinctively grabbed one of the animal's trailing reins.

Showing remarkable strength for a woman, Mrs. Skeffington held the frightened horse as it dragged her away from the train. Before anyone could move to help her, two Comanches galloped in close and fired arrows into the old woman's chest.

Mrs. Skeffington stared at the Indians in outrage. Holding the rein with one hand, she raised her rifle with the other and blew a great gob of flesh from one Comanche's shoulder. The startled Indians turned their horses and raced back to their comrades.

As Jake and Molyneaux raced out to her, the old woman shook her rifle at the Indians. "You beasts! How dare you!"

Jake grabbed her arm to steady her, wondering why she wasn't dead. "Let me help you, ma'am. Ain't you . . . ain't you hurt?"

"Hurt?" she replied indignantly, shaking him off. "Of course I'm not hurt." One of the arrows was embedded over her heart, the other was just below it.

The Indians' gunfire died away. They stopped yelling. There was an audible murmur from their massed ranks. Jake saw Yellow Wolf and his painted warriors pointing at the gray-haired woman with the arrows in her chest.

Molyneaux took the horse's rein from Mrs. Skeffington, who turned and walked back to her place in line as though nothing had happened. Others gathered around her, both worried and mystified. Essex reached for the top button of her dress, saying, "Here, let's take a look at that."

She smacked his hand away. "I beg your pardon, young man."

As Essex stepped back in surprise, Mrs. Skeffington began to undo her dress. Then she stopped. "What's the matter?'' she snapped at the openmouthed onlookers. ''Haven't you ever seen a lady's corset before?''

There were murmurs, then laughs, as everyone realized why she hadn't been killed. She eased the arrows from the tough whalebone corset, then she carefully pulled them through the holes in her dress, so as not to tear it further.

''Look!'' said Harvey Reed, pointing.

The Indians had stopped circling. They were moving off to the flanks. They were retiring. Instead of a final rush, they faded away, and the wagon train found itself alone on the plain.

''Well, I'm damned,'' Essex said, watching the Indians leave.

Woodhouse had come up, battered silk hat cocked over one eye. ''I expect the Comanches consider Mrs. Skeffington to be what you chaps call 'bad medicine,' '' he said.

Jake watched the old woman reloading her rifle. ''I expect they're probably right.''

13

Jake looked at his little command. There was more than an hour of daylight left, but these people were in no condition to go farther. Men and animals were panting with thirst and exhaustion. There was no water here, but at least the animals—those that would eat it—could graze on the dried bunch grass.

"We'll go into camp here," he said. "Circle the wagons. Unhitch the teams and let them graze while it's still light."

Wearily, the emigrants dragged the remaining wagons into a circle. Jake helped Essex and Woodhouse with their team. Then he detailed sentries and set the guard rotation. He got some salve from Mrs. Skeffington, rubbed his burned hand with it, and wrapped the hand with a length of bandage, holding the loose end in his teeth to keep it tight. A number of the emigrants had received minor wounds and scrapes, but no one was seriously hurt.

Jake went once around the camp. Culpepper was attending the wounded animals. Cutter, bathed in sweat, was greasing a squealing axle spindle. McWilliams and Hart were hammering wooden wedges under Webb's iron tires to tighten them. Big George Lambert was fitting a new popper to his long bullwhip. Hampton had started a fire, and some of the men were cutting up a mule to cook, while others fried cornmeal mush. Still others, like Ross and old Grinstead, were already asleep, sprawled on the ground as if dead, snoring. Incredibly, the Cutter children were playing fetch with their dog.

Jake unsaddled his horse. He gave him some coffee-water from his hat and fed and hobbled him. Then he took his rifle and walked to the highest point around, a low eminence about a hundred yards away. Nowak was on sentry there. Jake nodded to him. "All quiet?"

"As a graveyard."

Jake looked out. There was no sign of the Comanches. Jake could never understand how they vanished like that, like ghosts. He wondered what Yellow Wolf was saying to them now. The Indians had lost at least four men today and no telling how many horses. Like the whites, they had used a lot of ammunition. Some, if not many, of the braves must have exhausted their supplies of arrows, powder, and ball—supplies that were hard for them to come by. Water would be a problem for them, too. It had been a long day for the Comanches, and they had nothing to show for it. Jake was sure there would be arguments around the campfires for them to quit now, for them to take their scalps and stolen horses and return to Comancheria. The two sides were at stalemate. If the whites could not afford another day like this, neither could the Comanches.

The sun was setting as Jake walked back to camp and sank wearily down by the fire. He began cleaning his rifle. His messmates had left him some pinole fried with bacon. He ate as he worked, washing down the mixture of Mexican corn, spices, and dried beef with coffee-water from his canteen. Across from him, Woodhouse was sketching. Essex was off being sergeant of the guard.

Jake worked an oily patch down the rifle barrel with his ramrod. He struggled to keep his eyes open. His burned hand throbbed, and he cursed himself for being stupid enough to have grabbed a hot rifle barrel.

"Interesting day, eh?" Woodhouse said. The Englishman held his pad at arm's length, contemplating his work.

Jake snorted. "If that's what you want to call it. Personally, I wish I'd had the money to take a ship to California.''

"Always wanted to ask you, old man. How did you manage to diddle away all that bonus Army pay? Surely El Paso wasn't that expensive. Lost it at poker, did you?''

Jake cleaned out his weapon's fouled breech. "I . . . I had most of my pay advanced before we left San Francisco. I needed it for . . . for a girl.''

Woodhouse smiled broadly. "Ah ha, now the truth comes out. I should have suspected something of the sort.''

"This girl is seven years old," Jake said. "Her parents was burned to death." He held out his scarred hands. "Same fire I got these. I'm sort of her . . . her godfather. She starts convent school this year, and she needs the money for tuition and such.''

Woodhouse raised an eyebrow. "You don't really expect me to believe that, do you?''

"Believe what the hell you like. I'd never have taken the damn Army's scouting job if I hadn't needed that bonus money.''

Jake finished with his rifle, then cleaned his revolvers. When that was done, he went to the wagon and filled his Army cartridge boxes along with the smaller box that held percussion caps. He made another round of the sentries. Then at last he could get his blanket from the wagon, unroll it, and lie down, removing his pistol belt and boots. His eyelids felt like they were made of cement.

Woodhouse passed him something. "Here.''

It was the sketch. It showed a bearded scarecrow, dressed in rags, wearing two revolvers and holding a rifle. The tattered figure was standing against an empty horizon, forlorn yet heroic. In the background were some canvas-topped wagons.

"What is it?" Jake said.

"It's you.''

Jake looked again. "I don't look that bad, do I?''

"Actually I've been rather generous with you. Take it, it's yours."

Jake stared at the picture of himself for a long moment. Then he folded it carefully and placed it inside his red flannel shirt. "Thanks," he said.

The Englishman's eyes were closed; he was already half asleep. "Don't mention it," he murmured.

Jake laid his head on his saddle. He shut his eyes.

He seemed to be in a bottomless black void, falling. Rising to meet him, he saw the face of Yellow Wolf, painted with black stripes. He saw Bobby Durham, looking over his shoulder in terror. He saw Willinsky and Israel Combs. He saw Red Horse waving a feathered lance with a scalp on it—Jake's scalp. He heard shots and screams of pain that might have been his own, and somebody was shaking him, calling his name.

"Jake, Jake! Wake up!"

Jake opened his eyes. He was covered with sweat. He wasn't even sure he'd been asleep, yet it was pitch dark, and there was Dan Essex shaking his shoulder, and behind Essex was Sloane with a lantern.

With a thick tongue, Jake mumbled, "What is it?"

"Cutter's ill," Essex said. "It looks like cholera."

14

Jake stumbled along behind Essex and Sloane. Woodhouse was wakened by the commotion, and he came with them. Others of the company were awake as well.

"He's been up an hour," Essex said. "I was hoping it was just an attack of dysentery, but he's begun vomiting, too."

"What time is it?" Jake asked. He was so tired, he felt as if he were in a dream. His eyes didn't want to focus. He just wanted to lie down and sleep. He wanted all this to go away.

"Bit after ten," Essex told him. "Afraid it's going to be another long night."

There were already a number of people around Cutter's small wagon, keeping well back. By the lantern's light, Jake saw the grizzled farmer doubled over, on his side in a pool of his own mire. He vomited a watery paste. "Oh, God," he moaned, "my arms and legs hurt." His distraught wife, Melissa, was kneeling beside him, hugging him and bathing his face with a damp cloth. His children cringed in Mrs. Boone's skirts.

"It's cholera, all right," Jake said. "Or something so like it as not to make a difference."

"It's that damned water," Essex swore. "I knew it was no good."

"What bloody choice did we have?" Woodhouse said. "It was drink that or die of thirst."

By now, most of the company had gathered around. Jake

tried to remember the treatment for cholera. "We need calomel and mustard plasters, if we got any."

"And a teaspoon of brandy every half hour," spoke up Mrs. Skeffington. "I've been through this before. Too many times. We'll need camphor, as well, though I've only a bit of that. And Mr. Cutter will need his stomach rubbed, to lessen the cramps."

"I'll do that," his wife said.

"I'll help," Mrs. Boone offered.

"We'll take turns," Jake said. He didn't want to rub Cutter's stomach. He didn't want to be anywhere near a cholera victim, but he was the leader. He was expected to set an example. "Everybody else keep away from him." Cholera was contagious, though no one knew how it was transmitted. The best guess was that it traveled in invisible clouds with the breath, so Jake made sure that everyone treating the sick man covered their faces.

Essex was right. It was a long night. Few men slept. Most sat staring at one another uncomfortably, wondering who would get the disease next. They listened to Cutter's agonized groans, to his sputterings and cries for water.

Around midnight, Cutter's two children fell ill. Then their aunt, Mrs. Boone. Some of the emigrants were beginning to tell themselves that the disease would confine itself to the one family, when, in the early morning hours, red-haired Jim Hart stumbled in from his sentry post. "I've got it, boys. Oh, Lord, I've got it. Rub me down. Rub me. Oh, Lord, it hurts."

By the time dawn spread its bleak light across the desert, Sloane and the Alabama boy Ethan Andrews were ill as well, though their cases seemed milder than the others. The rest of the emigrants looked like walking dead from lack of sleep. For the moment, however, fear was subordinated and routine took over. There was breakfast to be eaten, teams to be grained and hitched.

"We'll have to leave the sick," Tyler Hampton said as

cook fires crackled against the gray sky. "If they get better, they can catch up."

The choice was tempting. It was risky to endanger the health of the others by bringing the sick along. "No one gets left," Jake said. "Not in this country."

"Goddamn it, Moran. You bring them along and you'll kill the whole company. They're going to die anyway, it's stupid to—"

"I don't care," Jake said. "They deserve a chance, and they're going to get it."

There was angry muttering and shuffling of feet from the men nearby. A lot of them disagreed with Jake this time. He said, "The Cutters will ride in their wagon at the rear of the train. We'll need a second wagon for the other sick."

"They can have mine," Mrs. Skeffington said. There were dark circles under the old woman's eyes from staying awake all night.

"That means we got to dump all the food that's in them two wagons," protested Blade. "Won't be no room for the sick otherwise, and the other wagons can't haul no extra weight."

"If that's what we have to do, that's what we'll do," Jake said testily. He was tired of arguing. His sleeves were rolled up; his scarred forearms and his clothes were permeated with the nauseous cholera smell. His shoulders and hands ached from rubbing cramped stomachs and limbs.

Mrs. Skeffington went on, "I'll ride with the sick men. Someone has to look after them."

Jake regarded her steadily. "You realize the risk, ma'am?"

"This is not the first time I've run it, Captain."

"Very well. You'll need a teamster."

The men looked at each other. No one was eager to drive the cholera wagon.

"I'll do it," Culpepper said, limping forward.

"The devil you will!" protested his owner, Molyneaux.

"Your duty is to my wagon, to *our* wagon. I can't afford to lose you."

"I don't see nobody else volunteerin', Langdon," Jake said. "*You* want to do it?"

Molyneaux went pale. He gulped.

Jake said, "The job's yours, Culpepper."

"He's your nigger, Langdon," Hampton said. "Don't let Moran tell you what to do with him."

Molyneaux hesitated, but he did not press the matter.

"Bah," Hampton said, turning away in disgust.

"Who'll drive Cutter's wagon?" Essex asked.

Culpepper scratched his bearded jaw. "I been thinkin' on that, Lieutenant. Long's the country's flat thisaway, we'n take the oxes off Mr. Cutter's rig and chain it to Miss Skeffington's. We got us extra mules from that wagon we left yesterday. Hitch eight to Miss Skeffington's, and they should pull 'em both along right smart like."

"Those are my mules," Hampton said, turning back. "No damn nigger's going to—"

"Sounds good to me," Jake told Culpepper, cutting off the enraged Carolinian in mid-sentence. "Get McWilliams, Nowak, and Reed to help you."

While the two sick-wagons were being chained together, Mrs. Skeffington canvassed the other wagon for spare shirts and underclothes and bolts of cloth to use as rags. She drew coffee-water from the dwindling supply in the casks. Finally, Jake, Essex, Woodhouse, and Culpepper—the only men who would touch them—lifted the sick people in, packing them in the seven-by-three wagon beds, where they would spill their body wastes over one another. Jake wished they could use a third wagon, but they couldn't afford to dump that much more food.

The wagons started off. They kept the same formation as yesterday, save for the two sick-wagons bringing up the rear. The men walked, to save the horses. Despite the repaired wheels, Webb's wagon still had trouble keeping up. They had not been on the trail an hour when Molyneaux

came down with the cholera and was jammed into the mal-
odorous sick-wagon with Hart, Sloane, and Andrews.

The sun rose in the cloudless blue sky. Across the wide
horizon, there was no sign of the Comanches, but Jake had
given up hoping that they'd gone away. The emigrants were
entering the worst part of their journey. Aside from Comanche Crossing—which could not be reached till late tomorrow—there was no guaranteed water until they got to
Hueco Tanks, thirty miles outside El Paso. They passed
more abandoned wagons. They passed the skeletons of
long-dead animals. By noon, Jake had counted four grave
markers. There was no telling how many more graves went
unseen or had been trampled over to keep them from the
Indians.

The pace was agonizingly slow. Twenty miles a day, the
standard for wagons, was beyond this company. They
trudged along in dust up to their ankles; great clouds of
dust billowed over them. The wagon wheels sank in the
dust, and the animals had to be whipped along. The dust
made the emigrants' throats raw; it irritated their skins and
made them erupt with sores. Most of them suffered from
dysentery; all were wracked with thirst. The coffee-water
had been scarcely potable when it was first made; now it
was stale and rank and turning green in the casks. The
water was infected, but they had to drink it. It was a choice
between possible death from cholera and certain death by
thirst.

The walkers tried not to listen to the wrenching noises
from the sick-wagons. They tried not to breathe the stench.
When Cutter's wife could take no more and had to leave
the wagon for some fresh air, Mrs. Skeffington divided her
time between the two groups of sick, moving from one
wagon to the other. She sopped up the foul mess with rags.
She gave her patients brandy and calomel, and she rubbed
them tirelessly. She sang to keep up their spirits.

Not long after noon, the cholera claimed its first victim.
Nine-year-old Richard Cutter, so brave in yesterday's bat-

tle, slipped into a coma and died. He was followed quickly
by his sister Rachel. Usually cholera took a couple of days
to kill, but the emigrants were so weakened by thirst and
exhaustion and malnutrition that the disease worked its fatal course more rapidly.

Mrs. Skeffington wrapped the small bodies in canvas,
and they were laid in shallow graves. The company sang
the hymn of the Texas pioneers, "Shall We Gather at the
River." Mrs. Cutter, who had been so strong throughout
the ordeal, broke down. She began shrieking, "My babies!
Oh, God, my babies! Why? Why?"

Mrs. Skeffington put her arms around the sobbing woman
and held her close. "Go ahead and cry, dear. Let it come.
It's good for you. I know how you feel. I lost both my
own children to fever in Florida, during the Seminole
Wars."

The emigrants started back to their places in line. The
usually insouciant Woodhouse was shaken. "My God. Less
than a day ago they were playing with the dog. Now . . ."

"It won't be the same without them," Essex said.

"Funny, ain't it?" Jake said. "One reason Cutter headed
for California was to get away from the malaria in them
East Texas bottomlands. Now he's lost his kids to a disease
a hell of a lot worse than malaria."

"He'll be joining them soon, I'm afraid," Essex said.

Jake nodded. The farmer had voided all the liquid in his
body. The cramps and dry heaves were tearing him apart
inside. He seemed to have shrunk to half his once robust
size. The veins around his mouth, across his forehead, and
down his neck were dark blue, where they'd broken inter-
nally from the strain of the constant vomiting. His skin was
cold and wrinkled, and it stayed where it was when
pinched. His pulse could scarcely be felt. Molyneaux, Hart,
and Mrs. Boone were much the same. Ethan Andrews and
Frank Sloane suffered the same symptoms but to a lesser
degree.

The party continued their nightmare march. One of the

oxen lay down and died. Then another. Mess Number 1, the wagon Jake shared with Woodhouse and Essex, was abandoned. The other wagons threw out 100-pound sacks of corn and sides of bacon to ease the strain on their animals. The ribs of Molyneaux's thoroughbred were showing; his coat was dull. There were sores on his flanks, and he'd begun to hobble.

During the afternoon, Cutter's cramps lessened. He became calm, peaceful. Shortly after, he died. This time there were no hymns at the burial. The company had grown too numb for hymns. They had grown too used to death. Cutter's sister-in-law, Mrs. Boone, died next. When she was buried, the Cutter wagon was abandoned. It was infected. No one wanted it or the few goods it still contained. Mrs. Cutter walked along with the remaining wagons, bonnetless, her eyes glazed in shock.

"Poor woman," murmured Woodhouse. "Her entire family, gone in a day. What reason has she to live?"

"Goin' to California's prob'ly the best thing for her now," Jake said. "There's plenty of men out there. She'll have more marriage offers than she can handle within a week after we reach gold country. If she's ever to get over what's happened, this'll be the way."

It was a subdued company that circled into camp that evening. There was no water, but there was thin, sere grass for the animals. McWilliams shot some jackrabbits and cooked them Ranger style, laying them on hot embers, turning them every minute or so, and flaking off the done pieces. Mrs. Skeffington took some of the meat and bones, and, with some of the remaining coffee-water, she made a broth for the sick men.

The surviving patients—Hart, Molyneaux, Andrew, and Sloane—were laid in the open air, off to themselves. Mrs. Skeffington leaned against the tail board of her wagon. She pressed her fingers against her eyes, which were swollen from exhaustion and lack of sleep. She was sweaty and foul-smelling, splashed with filth and vomit. The bluish tint was gone from her gray hair, which hung loose and lank. She had discarded her corset, giving her matronly figure freedom of movement. She was a far cry from the prim and proper woman who had once complained about the men spitting tobacco juice within the circle of wagons, where the ladies might step in it. The filthy rags that she had used to clean out the wagon were burning in an evil-smelling pile.

"Best eat," Jake told her. "Then get yourself some sleep."

She straightened with a jerk, shaking her head and blinking. "I will. I—I've just a bit more to do here."

"No, you go on. I'll watch them awhile."

She started to protest, but he took her shoulder and steered her away.

"You'd better look at Mr. Molyneaux first," she told him.

There was not much left of the handsome Georgia dandy now. Molyneaux had shrunken into himself. His veins were horribly swollen and discolored. His expensive clothes were rags. His hair and beard were matted with filth. His eyes were sunken, his breath sickening. He was calm, though, breathing with a light shudder. Culpepper sat beside him, giving him water from his canteen, a few drops to make his last minutes easier. The slave had taken off his glazed hat. His lips were pursed with compassion—with sorrow, even. Molyneaux looked up at him hopefully, as if Culpepper could do something to prevent the inevitable.

Jake knelt beside them. Molyneaux grinned at him; his cadaverous face was yellow beneath his tan. "Get the cards from my coat," he joked. "We have . . . we have time for a hand or two yet."

A short while later, Jake walked slowly back to the main camp. "Molyneaux's dead," he said.

The burial was quick. Jake and Culpepper dug the hole— there were only two shovels left in the company. Essex and Woodhouse laid the body in. The rest of the emigrants watched dully; many were too weary to stand.

The last spadeful of earth was thrown onto the grave. Jake and Culpepper lingered a moment in the fading heat, holding their hats. "He weren't so bad," Culpepper said in a low voice. "He just didn't know no better."

Culpepper stayed. When two men have spent so much of their lives together, even as adversaries, it takes a long time to say goodbye. Jake put on his hat and started away. He found Tyler Hampton blocking his path, grinning.

"This leaves us an interesting problem," Hampton said.

Jake stared. He was dull-eyed, defeated.

Hampton said, "What do we do with Molyneaux's nigger?"

15

"What?" said Jake, puzzled.

"He's property," Hampton said. "How do we dispose of him?"

Woodhouse was standing nearby. "Property?" he said. "Good God, man, surely you don't mean—"

"Don't I? His deed is in Molyneaux's wagon. I suggest you read the company articles concerning the property of members who die."

Most of the others, save those on sentry duty and Mrs. Cutter, had gathered around. In the west, the sun was going down.

"What are you getting at?" Jake said. He was dead beat. He was thirsty. He was worried about the sick men. He glanced over his shoulder at Culpepper. The tall slave stood watching impassively.

"I'm officially calling the company to order," Hampton said. "Webb, what are our options regarding this nigger?"

The flaxen-haired company secretary pushed his glasses up on his nose. "The way I see it, Tyler, we have two choices. We can sell this chattel among ourselves—auction him, if you like—with the proceeds going to Langdon Molyneaux's family in Georgia."

"But the proceeds might also be split among ourselves, right?" Hampton said.

"Yes, I suppose they might. This is a question for the company to decide. The other option would be for us to sell him in Tucson—they have a small slave market, I believe. Once again, the proceeds would be distributed as the company thought best. We might perhaps realize a better price in Tucson, thought it would leave us the problem of who controls the nigra in the interim.''

''Tell you what,'' Hampton said. ''How many of us are left?'' He counted quickly. ''Sixteen? All right, I'll pay the company three thousand, two hundred for him. That's two hundred dollars in the pocket of every man and woman here. That'll go a long way toward making up the losses you all have suffered.''

''Such generosity is not for me, thank you,'' Mrs. Skeffington said. ''I'll take no profit from the sale of human life.''

''Nor I,'' said Dan Essex.

''Nor I,'' said Woodhouse. The Englishman looked like he wanted to add something, but he kept quiet, probably because he knew how touchy Americans were about slavery.

''Or me,'' Nowak said. The Czeck refugee was one of those who lacked the energy to rise from the ground. His once upswept mustache was ragged and drooping. ''Harvey Reed, he is on sentry, but he will not want this money, either. Or Mr. Hart, I think, or Frank Sloane.''

''Fine,'' laughed Hampton. ''That's more for everyone else.''

''How can you be so callous?'' Mrs. Skeffington said, sweeping a long strand of gray hair from her weary face. ''You're talking about a man who's helped this company a great deal.''

''I'm talking about a nigger, and I can do it because I have the law of the United States on my side,'' Hampton said.

''But why?'' Essex said.

''Let's just say I want to instill a proper attitude in him. I want to make him a more productive economic unit. Is that a good choice of terms, Blade?''

The overseer grinned through his dusty brown beard. ''I

don't know 'bout that, Cap'n, but I don't recollect none of the niggers we worked back in Carolina bein' so uppity. Taste of the lash'll take that out'n him real quick."

Jake saw Culpepper stiffen; he saw the slave's lips tighten with anger. Culpepper had no control over his own destiny. He could not fight what was happening to him. These men would think nothing of killing him.

"All this doesn't make sense, Hampton," Essex went on. "You can't even bring slaves into California."

"Call it a whim," Hampton said. "Call it an investment. Maybe I'll turn back for Texas. Maybe I'll sell the nigger when we hit Tucson and chance turning a profit on him there." He laughed. "Maybe I'll just leave him in the desert for the Indians, the way we've been leaving busted-up wagons and furniture and sacks of cornmeal."

He laughed again. Blade and the gold-toothed Missourian Ross laughed with him.'

"We must do something with him, you're right," Webb said. "Are you tending a formal offer, Tyler?"

"That's right," Hampton said.

"Is anyone prepared to better that offer?" Webb asked the company.

No one was.

"Does anyone prefer that we wait and sell the nigra Culpepper in Tucson?"

No one did.

"Then, Tyler, I suppose that—"

"You're forgetting one option," Jake said.

Hampton turned arrogantly. "What option?"

"We can set him free."

"What?" said Hampton, incredulous.

"You can't be serious," Blade said.

"Dead serious," Jake told them.

"We've no legal right to free him," Webb said, shaking his head. "Molyneaux made no mention of manumission before he died, and he left no will. And since we have a valid deed to the nigra, the matter would seem to be cut and—''

''I don't give a damn about deeds,'' Jake said. ''Culpepper's a man. We ain't sellin' him like some damn plow horse.''

''Good for you, Captain,'' applauded Mrs. Skeffington.

Essex grinned. Woodhouse nodded approvingly, along with Nowak. There was angry talk and shaking of heads from the rest of the men. Even old Grinstead, who was from Massachusetts, a state with a lot of abolitionist sentiment, was uncomfortable with the idea of a free Negro in the company.

Webb spoke earnestly, looking surprised. ''You're a Southron, Jake, like most of us here. You supportin' a nigra's freedom—it's like you betrayin' your own people.''

''That's right, Jake,'' big George Lambert said. ''I'm with you on most things, but . . . well, damn if I can see freein' no nigger. I never heard of such. Ethan, he ain't, neither.''

Jake was surprised himself. He was from a slave state; he'd been around slaves all his life. He'd taken slavery for granted. But this was a case about which he felt strongly. He wasn't sure why. Maybe it was the thought of Culpepper being owned by a man like Tyler Hampton.

''You're not insisting on this, I hope?'' Webb asked him.

''Hope again,'' Jake said.

''Care to put it to a vote?'' Hampton said smugly. There was angry approval. Hampton had finally found an issue to rally the majority of the company behind him.

''No votes,'' Jake said. ''You people elected me to lead you, and, by God, that's what I'm going to do. I say Culpepper goes free. He's earned it, if any man has. Molyneaux's wagon and everything in it are his as well.''

''Bullshit!'' shouted Blade.

''No!'' cried Lambert.

''You can't ride roughshod over us this way, Moran,''

swore Hampton. "You've given your last order to this company."

"If you don't like it, do something about it." Jake glared at Hampton. If they had to have it out, he was ready to do it now.

Hampton glowered, but he made no move.

"Anybody else?" Jake said, looking at the others.

No one challenged the Hero of Chapultepec.

"That's what I thought," Jake said.

He turned and started away. He hated this job. He was tired of everyone looking to him for direction and then feeling free to—

"Watch out, Jake!" shouted Essex. There was a sudden pain across Jake's chest and arms, like a razor slicing through them. It drew the breath from him in a great searing sob. Something gripped him, twisted him, and spun him loose, and he stumbled off balance and fell. In the back of his mind, he realized he'd been hit with a whip.

He lay on his hands and knees, stunned with pain. His shirt was torn; he felt blood running down his arms and chest. He heard a crack, and there was a knifing agony across his back that drew him into the air with a scream. He fell full length in the dust.

He looked up. Hampton was whirling a muleskinner's whip over his head. He must have grabbed it from the nearest wagon. Blade had Essex and Woodhouse covered with pistols. The whip snaked toward Jake. He ducked his head. There was an explosion above his left ear. He heard himself screaming. Blood spouted over his shoulder.

He curled up in a ball for protection. The whip cracked, and there was a pain on his spine that arched his back and made him scream again. He heard Hampton yelling, "Get up! Get up, damn you!"

The whip whistled as Hampton whirled it around and around his head. He was showing off, setting up the killer blow. Jake concentrated what strength he had left. He half scrambled, half crawled for the nearest wagon. Hampton saw. The whip caught Jake's ankle. It held him for a moment, then he desperately kicked it off. He dragged himself through the dirt and cowered beneath the relative safety of the wagon.

He lay there, sobbing with pain, gasping for breath. Tears ran down his cheeks. He saw Hampton's boots approaching. Hampton looked under the wagon at him. The dark round face was full of hate. He cracked the whip under, but Jake slid to the far side of the wagon. Bending over, Hampton couldn't get leverage with the whip, and the long black lash snaked harmlessly in the dirt.

Hampton ran to the other side of the wagon, but Jake rolled away again. Hampton could not get at him.

"Get out of there, Moran!"

Jake was shaking with pain; there was blood all over him. "Come and get me!" he cried.

He couldn't stay here. Hampton would think to get a gun any second. Jake had taken off his own pistols when they camped; he'd have to make a dash for them. He gathered himself. He rolled from under the wagon, away from his enemy. He stood, amid nauseating waves of pain. The blood drained from his head; he fought for breath.

Suddenly his arm was grabbed in a strong grip. Blade. He turned and tried to hit the overseer, but someone grabbed his other arm. It was Ross. The two men held him, struggling, arms pinned to his sides, helpless.

Hampton walked around the side of the wagon, coiling the long whip. His lips drew back from his yellow teeth in an evil grin. "You ruined me, Moran. Now I'm going to make you pay." He measured the distance to his target and shook out the whip. "Hold him steady, boys, I wouldn't want to miss. We'll try for an eye first."

He drew back the whip.

There was the click of a revolver hammer. "Leave him go," Dan Essex said. The ex-sailor's pistol was leveled at Hampton's head.

Ross and Blade dropped Jake's arms and went for their guns.

"You heard the gentleman," said Woodhouse. Ross and Blade turned, to find themselves looking down the barrel of the Englishman's rifle. "The first one of you chaps to move is dead. You have my promise on that."

Neither man moved.

Jake looked at Hampton's other man, McWilliams. But the Ranger was keeping out of this.

"It's over," Essex said. "There'll be no more. Hampton, we're placing you under arrest until we—"

"No," Jake said. "It ain't over." He moved out and raised his fists. "Come on, Hampton."

Essex said, "Jake, you're hurt. Don't—"

"Keep out of this, Dan." He motioned to Hampton. "Come on, you son of a bitch."

Hampton tossed aside the whip. He moved forward, his big fists clenched. "I'm going to beat the living hell out of you, Moran."

Jake had thought about this moment many times, even as he had prayed it wouldn't come. Hampton was heavier and stronger. Jake had to keep his distance. He had to wear the Carolinian down, then move in for the kill. He couldn't trade blows with Hampton; he couldn't let Hampton get him on the ground.

Hampton set himself, but before he could charge, Jake stepped in and hit him on the nose. He hit him again, rocking Hampton back. He was trying to break Hampton's nose. He hit Hampton with a left hand, then a right, knocking Hampton back again, but he was hurt and his punches lacked power.

Hampton shook his head, then he rushed in. Jake hit him flush in the face, but it didn't stop him. Hampton lowered his head, drove it into Jake's chest, and knocked him onto his back, slamming the air from his lungs. Jake lay gasping; his head was spinning. He was being hit in the face. Hit again. He'd be killed if he stayed on the ground with

Hampton on top of him. He reached up and dug his fingers into Hampton's face, shoving him back, working on Hampton's exposed belly with his other hand. Punches rained on his jaw, on his shoulder. He grabbed a handful of hair and desperately kicked the bigger man off him.

They rolled over and over, legs tangled, pushing each other's faces into the dirt, grunting with effort, gouging and kicking and clawing, doing anything they could to hurt the other. Hampton aimed a knee at Jake's groin, missed, and came down hard on the inside of Jake's thigh, making his leg go numb. They rolled up against a wagon wheel. Hampton grabbed Jake's head and began banging it against the metal wheel hub, trying to crack it open. Jake jabbed a finger hard into Hampton's left eye.

"Ow!" Hampton yelled. He dropped Jake and held his eye.

Jake punched the big man aside and staggered to his feet. He doubled over, catching his breath, while Hampton rose unsteadily. Hampton's chest was rising and falling heavily; his face was red with unwonted exertion. The eye was already swelling shut.

Jake raised his fists, determined this time to keep away, to follow his plan. Hampton moved close. He swung a booted foot at Jake's crotch. Jake jumped aside, and Hampton hit him with a fist on his injured ear.

Hampton grinned as Jake staggered and winced. Jake saw the dark, round face; he saw the beady eyes, the hint of freckles. He thought of the whip. He thought of all the insults he'd taken from Hampton's big mouth, and suddenly he lost control of himself. He forgot his plan, and with a snarl he leaped at Hampton, fists swinging.

He stood toe to toe with the bigger man, exchanging punches. He was doing exactly what he hadn't wanted to do, and he didn't care. He felt himself being hit, being rocked, and it only made him hit out harder. He knew he was hurt, but the fighting madness carried him away, and he didn't feel the pain. Again and again he hit at the big face, feeling it crunch beneath his fists, watching it dissolve in blood, until the face was no longer there. He swung at empty air, lost his balance, and almost fell. He looked around. Tyler Hampton was lying at his feet. Hampton's face was puffed and bloody; his half-open mouth was filled with blood. He rolled his head from side to side, gurgling and moaning softly, unable to rise.

Jake stumbled, wobbly. His lungs were screaming for air. Thirst burned his throat. His face flowed with sweat. He wiped away the sweat and discovered it was blood. There was a gash under his eye. The back of his head hurt; his jaw hurt. His right hand was throbbing horribly. He flexed it, fearing the worst, but it was not broken. He must have bruised the bones. His red flannel shirt hung from him in strips.

He stood over Hampton. He had never hated a man so much in his life. He wanted to finish the job; he wanted to kick Hampton's fat face to jelly, but he restrained himself. He couldn't put himself on Hampton's level.

He looked around. "Webb, draw up a paper." It hurt to talk; it hurt to breathe. It was hard to concentrate, but he made himself do it. "Make it say Culpepper's free. Make it for my signature as captain. You witness it and put an entry in the company log. Then give the paper and the deed of property to Mr. . . ." He turned to Culpepper. "What *is* your last name, anyway?"

"Ain't got one," said the black man.

"Pick one."

Culpepper shrugged. "Smith."

"Give it to Mr. Smith." Jake reeled as waves of pain swept over him. He couldn't keep his eyes focused.

Culpepper's pride made him defiant. "I reckon you expect me to thank you?"

"Not particularly," Jake said.

Jake felt himself falling, and he steadied himself. More than anything in the world, he wanted to lie down. He wanted to sleep. But he could not, not with everyone watching.

He straightened. He forced himself to turn, slowly, so that he would not fall. Essex reached out to help him, but Jake shrugged him off. He had to do this himself. He walked away, with the eyes of the company on him. He had won, but he knew that his troubles with Hampton were not over. He could only guess what would happen next.

16

Just before dawn, five pistol shots sounded in quick succession through the camp.

The emigrants tumbled from their blankets, shouting, "What is it? Are the Indians attacking?" A nervous sentry—Lambert—fired his rifle into the darkness, adding to the confusion.

Dan Essex was sergeant of the guard. "Battle stations!" he yelled, forgetting for a moment that he was no longer at sea. "Don't fire until you have a target!"

The men grabbed their weapons and went to their places. There were no more shots.

"Anybody see anything?" Essex shouted. "Sentries?"

"Them shots came from the wagons," cried McWilliams from his guard post.

"What? Are you sure?"

"Sure as I'll ever be, Lieutenant."

Essex looked around. Every figure was out of his blankets. Every figure but one.

"Jake!"

Essex hurried over. Jake's blanket was still rolled around his recumbent figure. His hat still lay on the saddle at its head. As Essex drew close, he saw five small, ragged holes in the blanket, placed together in a close pattern.

"Oh, no."

Essex bent down and pulled the blanket away—revealing two 100-pound sacks of cornmeal laid end to end. Trickles of corn spilled out of one sack, where the five bullets had ripped into it.

"What the—?"

Someone chuckled, and everyone turned as Jake Moran stepped out of the shadows beyond the wagons.

Jake wore a blue shirt that Culpepper had given him from Molyneaux's effects. His torn trousers were mended as best he could, though the knees were completely gone. A lit *cigarito* dangled from his mouth. He hurt all over—his head, his face, his hand. The whip cuts on his back and chest were smeared with the last of Mrs. Skeffington's salve. There was a bandage over his left ear.

"Oldest trick in the book," Jake said, grinning at the startled faces of Essex and the others, "but it still works. I was expecting something like this to happen."

"Did you see who shot at your blanket roll?" Essex said.

"Didn't get a good look, but it ain't hard to guess." Jake turned. "What's wrong, Hampton? Surprised to see me alive?"

By the dim light of the campfire, Hampton looked suddenly pale. His guilt was plain. Hampton's left eye was purpled shut. His face was lumpy and embittered. He slurred his words through puffed lips, "What do you mean?"

"Did you do it yourself?" Jake asked. "Or didn't you have the guts? Who'd you send? Ross? Blade?"

"Hey, it wasn't me," Ross said.

"Don't drag me into this," Blade said, backing off.

Hampton recovered some of his swagger. "What if it was me, Moran? What are you going to do about it? Call me out?"

"That's exactly what I'm doing," Jake said.

He had no choice. Everyone knew who had fired those shots. He had to revenge himself, or he'd lose all his authority, all his respect. This had nothing to do with the company. This was personal. No one would try to talk him out of this.

He could see Hampton's confidence growing. He knew that Hampton had been in pistol duels before—that's why he'd been kicked out of the South Carolina Militia. Jake, on the other hand, had never been in such an affair, despite what most of the company probably believed.

He couldn't let anyone know the truth, though, especially Hampton. He couldn't give Hampton more of an edge than he already had. He had to act like he welcomed this. In a minute, he'd probably be dead. Well, that's what honor was all about.

He took a last drag on the *cigarito* and tossed it away. "You got a pistol that's still loaded, Hampton?"

Hampton brushed aside the skirt of his coat, revealing a pair of revolvers in his belt. "I have one."

"Better use it, then."

"Shall we name seconds? Do you want to stand back to back? Do you want someone to give us a count?"

"Just pull your piece and start shooting," Jake told him. "That's the way we do it out here."

Everyone backed up, under cover of the wagons. Jake's hand tensed over his pistol butt. God, his hand hurt. He eyed Hampton, waiting for him to make the first move.

Hampton's smile widened.

He was going to do it now.

"What's that?" Woodhouse said suddenly. "It smells like smoke."

Jake smelled it, too. It was smoke. Everyone was turning.

"My God—look!" old Grinstead said.

Jake saw Hampton's eyes leave him and stare off to the northwest. Jake hesitated, then he turned with the others. Bright flames were visible about a half mile off, licking at the darkness. Even as they watched, the flames spread across the horizon in a ragged line.

"What is it?" Woodhouse said.

"Comanches," Jake said grimly. "They're setting fire to the prairie."

17

The fire crackled toward the wagons; its wavering orange and yellow flames were hypnotic in the pre-dawn darkness. The smell of smoke grew heavier; the first wisps drifted around the watching emigrants. Beyond the advancing flames could be seen a series of larger, stationary fires. The familiar yells of the Comanches split the air.

"We're going to be burned alive!" cried Webb. "We've got to get out of here!"

Jake tried to put himself in Yellow Wolf's place; he tried to figure out what the old chief was up to. "I don't think so," he said. "This grass is too thin for that. They're burning it to try and scare us out of our circle. See them other fires? Probably they've brought bundles of dried brush from miles around. They're burning them for a smoke screen. They'll come in behind the smoke, waiting for us to try and get clear of the fire. They'll strike out of the smoke and darkness, and we'll never know what hit us."

"So what do we do?" babbled Grinstead. The onrushing fire was unnerving the men, just as Yellow Wolf had intended.

Jake was as scared as any of them—probably more scared than most—but he couldn't let it show. They thought him fearless, and he had to act that way for their sakes. "Don't panic, for one thing. Go to your places. Double leash the animals to the wagons. Saddle the horses; cross-hobble them and the mules." He wished the animals could be blindfolded, as well, but there was not enough cloth, not enough time.

The men hurried off, forgetting the interrupted pistol duel. Hampton didn't forget, though. He was still ready to shoot it out. It was up to Jake.

Jake cast his eyes down, swallowing his pride for the good of the company. "Look, Hampton, I need your help too much to continue this—this thing between us. I'm willing to forget it if you are."

The big Carolinian stared at him. The dark eyes were as full of hate as ever. "Forget? No way. Call it a truce, instead. And let me tell you now, Moran—the minute this is over, I'm going to kill you."

Jake forced himself to look Hampton in the eye. He forced himself to smile. "You can try," he said.

"I will," promised Hampton, and he moved off.

In his wake came young Ethan Andrews from the sick-wagon. Ethan looked wan, but he was smiling. "I'm ready for duty now, Cap'n."

Jake put Hampton from his mind. "Good," he said, clapping Ethan on the shoulder. "Glad to have you back. Get your weapons. How's the others?"

Ethan's smile faded. "Sloane, he's better. But Mr. Hart's fell into a coma."

Jake nodded, and Ethan moved off.

The smoke from the burning grass was all around them now, rolling down on the breeze, thickened by the heavier smoke from the piles of burning brush. The smoke filled men's lungs and nostrils; it made them cough. The horses reared as the men tried to hobble them. They plunged and neighed wildly. The mules kicked and brayed with fear. The oxen lowed plaintively and tugged at their tethers. In the darkness behind the smoke, the Comanches yelled. They were getting ready to attack.

The emigrants watched in horrified fascination as the grass fire burned relentlessly toward the camp. There was no time for a fire break. There was no time even to shoot a horse and drag it back and forth in front of the wagons, beating down the grass. The flames moved in irregular lines, fierce and high in some places, in other places not burning at all because of a lack of grass. Then the flames were on them. They flickered under the wheels of the first wagon, but they consumed the thin, tinder-dry grass too quickly to set the wagon afire. The flame flickered around the men's boots and under the wildly stamping hooves of the animals, who were maddened by fire and smoke, maddened by the Indians yelling in the background. They strained at their tethers. One of the horses managed to get free, despite the cross-hobbles, and it disappeared downwind.

Sparks shot into the air; other sparks were borne on the breeze from the brush fires, glowing like tiny rockets. They landed on the backs of animals and men, burning until they were beaten out with coats and shirts and hats. A spark landed atop Hampton's wagon. The canvas top had been painted for waterproofing, and it was highly flammable. As men rushed to extinguish the spark, the canvas sputtered and began to burn. Ross—perhaps trying to atone for wrecking Hampton's other wagon in the ravine—climbed onto the wagon's small front wheel. He hoisted himself to the edge of the wagon bed, holding on to one of the hoops. He reached upward and beat at the spreading flames with his jacket. Then he was hit between the shoulder blades by an arrow. He held on. He kept beating his jacket at the flames, as if by reflex. Another arrow drove into the base of his spine. He waved the jacket wildly, beating nothing but air now. Then he fell to the ground.

Before another man could take his place, the flames had spread too far across the painted canvas to be put out. "There's ammunition in there!" Jake yelled. "Push the wagon out before it blows the rest of the wagons with it!"

Through the choking smoke, Jake raced with some others. He could not tell who they were, save for Essex. The Indians were attacking; he heard their yells, heard the whir of their arrows. With his bowie knife he whacked at the leather reins tying the mules and horses to the wagon. There was no telling where the freed beasts ran, no time to worry about it.

"Come on!" he yelled. He lifted the tongue of Hampton's wagon. The canvas top was a mass of flames. The heat was fierce on him; he could hardly breathe for the heat and smoke. Essex was alongside him; Woodhouse, Mc-Williams, and Hampton, too. "Push!"

Slowly they backed the heavy wagon and turned it. They pulled it from the circle out onto the scorched prairie. They couldn't see where they were going because of the dense smoke. Somebody was alongside, covering them with pistols—Ethan. The wagon's bed was blazing now. The heat was intense; the ammuntion would go any second.

They were fifty yards out; their tongues lolled in the hot air and smoke. Their eyes were burning. "That's enough!" Jake cried. "Run!"

They dropped the wagon tongue and ran for the camp. They flattened themselves to the earth as the cartridges began going off—singly at first, then a box, then the whole supply. There was a great bang. A hot wind blew over the men, taking their breaths away, throwing fire and sparks and bits of burning debris high into the air. Woodhouse yelled as a flaming piece of wood landed on his leg. He beat it out with his silk hat.

Jake forced himself upright. "Back to the wagons!" he said in a cracked voice.

The weary man raised themselves and moved back. Jake helped Woodhouse. Hampton's burning wagon cast a bright glow through the pall of smoke that hung over everything. The Indians were all around them, shooting arrows and rifles. Jake saw Yellow Wolf's white horse, illumined by the flames like a creature from Hell. There were hideous war cries, the crash of rifles, the scream of animals as they were shot. The Indians were able to ride through the smoke right up to the gap in the circle of wagons, fire, and get away without being seen. All was confusion; men were shouting and screaming in panic. They were crying, praying. Jake saw old Grinstead crawling around in circles on his hands and knees, dripping blood, the lower half of his jaw shot away.

Dan Essex loomed up beside Jake, calm as ever, the peaked leather cap pulled low. "The company's turning into a mob. We have to do something or it's all over for us."

"Yeah." Jake had been thinking the same thing. He watched the thick smoke drifting down and wondered if the emigrants could make it work for them.

"Stay here, Dan. Take charge of the wagons."

"What are you going to do?"

Jake grinned. "Counterattack."

Quickly Jake made his way through the confusion of smoke and noise, searching out the men he wanted. "McWilliams, get a horse. Meet me by Webb's wagon. Make sure your pistols are loaded. Blade—you, too." A minute later they were all there—Woodhouse, Hampton, Nowak, and Lambert with the first two. They strained to hear Jake's words over the din. Some grabbed their canteens and took hasty sips of stale coffee.

"We're going to ride around this smoke and attack," Jake told them. "We'll hope to catch the Indians napping and hit them in the flank."

"Do these horses have a charge left in them?" Woodhouse said.

"There's no time to worry about that. Mount up and follow me."

They rode off, losing sight of the wagons and the Indians almost immediately. They had to hurry, before the camp was overrun. The gunshots and yells were muffled in the smoke behind them.

They galloped several furlongs across the line of drifting smoke. Jake prayed they had not been seen. He waved his men left, into the smoke. The horses shied and fought the reins; they wanted to turn downwind. From the corner of his eye, Jake saw Hampton smack his animal with the barrel of his pistol.

They were in the thickest part of the smoke now, blinded. Jake's heart pounded wildly; he had no idea what they would find when they came out. There might be a hundred Comanches waiting for them. His hand tightened on the grip of his Navy Colt.

Then they were through, into clear air for what seemed like the first time in ages. It was just dawn. The gray light was dim and cold on the prairie. To their left were piles of burning brush, with more brush being thrown on by mounted Indians. To the windward of the fires was a horde of milling Comanches. The Indians were confident, careless in their certainty of victory and scalps. Some were reloading firearms. Others were laughing as they emerged from the smoke. Jaw saw Yellow Wolf directing new parties to the attack. The flames from Hampton's wagon glowed.

In the dim light, the Indians hadn't noticed the small party of white men ride out of the smoke. "Form a line," Jake said. The men spread out. "Make very shot count," Jake told them, repeating what he'd heard a Texas Ranger captain say in Mexico. "Powder burn the bastards. And don't get in a chase with them. Remember what happened last time."

He waved his arm. "Let's go."

The seven men dug in their spurs. They raced down on the mass of Indians. The thunder of hooves grew loud in Jake's ears, drowning all other sounds. He surrendered himself to the pounding rhythm of his horse. He felt a queer, exhilarating pleasure in this hell-for-leather charge. He was no longer scared. All that was past now.

A furlong went by. They were gaining momentum with every step, and still they were not seen. McWilliams forged ahead, driven by his demons, scalps flapping at his belt, yelling his high-pitched Texas war cry. The fool would give them away, but it was too late to do anything about it now. Jake put his head lower on his galloping horse's neck; he held his cocked revolver upright. Around him, the other men were yelling, too. Woodhouse's silk hat blew off.

The Indians turned, alerted. They pointed, crying out with surprise and fear. Jake saw Yellow Wolf trying to rally them. Some followed him; others turned to run.

Less than a furlong to go. Time seemed to stand still. There was a keening wind in Jake's ears. Beside him, Nowak's horse suddenly collapsed. The Czech went crashing into the ground headfirst and his pistol discharged, but Jake couldn't spare a look.

He leveled his revolver. Yellow Wolf was too far back in the press to try for. He picked out an Indian directly ahead, face painted red and yellow and black, greased skin glistening. The Indian was wheeling his pony toward Jake, lowering his lance, trying to gain momentum, but there wouldn't be enough time.

Jake heard McWilliams's shotgun boom. Then the mass of Indians came at him with a rush, and he hurtled into them. He fired at his target. The painted Indian screamed and disappeared. He cocked his pistol and fired again, at an Indian who was trying to turn away, and he hit him in the back of the neck. The pistol's muzzle almost touched the brave.

The momentum of Jake's charge carried him deep into the mass of Comanches. He trusted his pony to keep going, to avoid crashing into another mount. All around were shouts and gunshots. He fired at an Indian in front of him, and was past before he knew whether he'd hit the man or not. Yells sounded loud in his ears. Something whirred by him, grazing his cheek. He fired at a young brave, saw him slump over his pony's neck, and wheel away.

Jake's horse slowed in the confused press of men and animals. Everything was dust and smoke and cries. Jake's blood lust was up. This made up for all they had suffered at the hands of these savages. He fired at a shadow in the fog. He fired again, and the hammer clicked on an empty chamber. He holstered the revolver and drew his second. A Comanche rode at him, lance leveled. Jake flipped sideways in the saddle to avoid the lance, almost fell out, straightened, and snapped a shot at the Indian but missed. A figure bore up on the right. Jake almost fired before he realized it was Woodhouse. The Englishman was pursuing someone. Then Jake was alone. The fight had opened up. He wheeled his horse and spurred him. He came alongside a brave with blood dripping down his arm. He fired twice, saw the Indian fall over but stay on his horse. There was an explosion near his ear, and he realized he'd been shot at, but when he turned, there was no assailant to be seen in the dust and smoke. He rode toward the noise of battle. Someone passed in front of him. He swerved his horse to avoid the figure, fired, but once again couldn't tell whether he'd hit anything.

Then, in front of him, he glimpsed a pure white horse. Yellow Wolf. Here was a chance to end the emigrants' torment for good. Jake spurred toward the Comanche war chief. Yellow Wolf saw him coming through the dust. For a second, their eyes met, and there was a flash of recognition on the Indian's proud face. Yellow Wolf's long lance was behind his back; he carried his bow. He shot an arrow at the same moment as Jake fired his last bullet. The old Indian's act must have made Jake flinch, for he missed. His momentum took him past Yellow Wolf, and he yanked hard on his horse's reins, wheeling the animal around. Yellow Wolf had turned and was riding after his fleeing braves. Jake spurred wildly after him, wanting to kill him. The Indian looked back over his shoulder at Jake. Jake broke out the revolver's empty cylinder as he rode. He fumbled a full cylinder from his shirt. He was about to snap it in when his horse suddenly veered—he never knew from what—and Jake grabbed the pommel to avoid being thrown. The cylinder fell from his hand. Cursing, he found himself riding after Yellow Wolf with an empty pistol. He had another loaded cylinder, but before he could find it in his shirt, the Indian had drawn away and was fast disappearing on his speedy horse.

Jake reined in, boiling with rage. He wanted to throw the pistol after the retreating Indian, but he restrained himself. He looked around. Only a few minutes had elapsed since they had emerged from the smoke. He'd come farther from the wagons than he'd intended. His tired, thirsty horse was blowing heavily. Sweat lathered the animal's flanks. Blood ran down the horse's neck from where he must have been grazed by a lance. Jake had never even seen the thrust.

Jake was tired, too. Sweat and smoke made his cuts burn. His body screamed for water, and he unslung his nearly empty canteen. Before him, dust trails were scattered over the landscape as the Indians retreated. Bodies of Indians and their horses lay everywhere. Jake's counterattack had done grim work. There was a bitter taste in his mouth, though, because he could have ended it with Yellow Wolf's death. He should have ended it. But he had failed. He heard the low moans of wounded braves, and he put them out of his mind, because he knew the wounded would have to be killed. His own men were scattered, too, either reined in like himself or walking their horses wearily back toward him. He saw Lambert slumped in the saddle, holding his leg.

He heard a distant shot. Across the prairie, he spotted a group of riders. Someone was still pursuing the Comanches. It was McWilliams. Jake saw a puff of smoke, saw an Indian fall from his horse, then heard the distant pop of the Ranger's pistol.

"Get back! Get back!" Jake yelled, standing in his stirrups and waving his hat. But McWilliams was too far away. He couldn't hear; and even if he could, Jake knew he would keep on riding, consumed by his desire to kill Indians, by his desire to avenge his family.

The buckskinned rider grew small in the distance. There

was the faint echo of his high-pitched Texas yell. Suddenly a larger group of Indians converged on him. McWilliams boldly rode at them and was lost to sight in a cloud of dust. Jake heard another pistol shot. When the dust cleared, McWilliams was being led off by the Indians, who were yelling in triumph.

Jake closed his eyes and swore silently.

18

From the wagons, Dan Essex ran to where Jake sat his horse. The ex-sailor was a ragged, powder-begrimed apparition. "Jake, you did it!" He slapped Jake's thigh. "I knew you'd find a way!"

The rest of the emigrants emerged from the smoke, happy to breathe fresh air again, gulping it down gratefully. "I never thought we'd get out of that one," said Harvey Reed, still trembling from the battle.

"A brilliant action," Webb told Jake, squinting through his dirty glasses. "Brilliant. I shall make this engagement my lead story when we reach San Francisco. I shall see that news of it reaches the East."

Ethan Andrews, weak from his illness and out of breath, grinned. "By gum, we just about showed 'em, didn't we? How many'd we kill?"

"Seventeen," replied Blade, who'd been riding around, counting. "Seventeen dead—or soon to be dead." He laughed.

"We sent plenty more riding out of here with lead in 'em, too," George Lambert said, grimacing. George was bent over in the saddle, holding his left leg, the lower half of which was wet with blood.

The emigrants were flushed with victory, heedless for the moment of the dangers that still lay before them. Their praise droned in Jake's ears. Jake had fallen into one of his black depressions. Here he was, the worst kind of failure, and these fools were congratulating him. How many

135

members of the company had died because of his actions so far? Nine? How many were yet to die? If he hadn't dropped that revolver cylinder, he would have killed Yellow Wolf. Their troubles would have been over—with the Comanches at any rate. He wondered if Yellow Wolf regretted letting him live. He felt a curious kinship with the old Comanche chief, as if the Indian's unfathomable act of mercy had somehow bonded them together.

The air was split by a drawn out, distant scream.

Everyone turned.

There was another scream, piercing, horrifying in its intensity.

"What is it?" Harvey Reed said, ashen-faced.

"A polecat?" Ethan said.

"It's McWilliams," Jake told them.

Hampton walked his horse closer; the horse was limping badly. Hampton's left eye was swollen shut. "Yeah, hero, what about McWilliams? Do we just let those red bastards have their way with him?"

"You got a better idea?" Jake snapped. "We can't go after him. That's what Yellow Wolf wants us to do. That's why he's making sure we hear him."

There was another scream. Then more, sounds like no human ever made. The men's enthusiasms at their victory soured. Jake's mood grew blacker. He tried not to think of what was happening to the Ranger. It was all Jake's fault. He never should have let McWilliams ride in the attack; he should have taken someone else. He should have known that McWilliams, once in contact with the Indians, would not be able to stop.

They couldn't just stay here and listen to McWilliams scream. "Let's get ourselves organized and go," Jake said. "Every minute we stay is a minute later we get to water. That could be the difference between life and dying of thirst. Lambert, how's that leg?"

The big blond looked confident. He was built like a rock, and he'd never been hurt before in his life. "Hell, I'll be all right.'' His thigh had been shattered by a rifle ball. He didn't feel any pain yet. He would.

"Will the Comanches be back?" asked Lambert's friend Ethan Andrews. He wasn't grinning anymore.

"Depends," Jake replied. "This was a big defeat for them. They have to go back now and make medicine, see what to do. We bought us some time, if nothing else."

On the way back to camp, they found Nowak. The mustachioed Czech was dead, his neck snapped by the fall from his horse. The gaunt horse had not been shot; it had simply died under him. Its heart had given out; it hadn't been able to take the strain of the charge. Jake unbuckled Nowak's revolver belt and slung it over his own saddle.

The sun was not yet up. The distant screams had stopped. The prairie was silent, save for the crackle of flames and the moans of wounded men and animals. The piles of brush still burned; their smoke billowed on the breeze. Dying flames enveloped Hampton's wagon, which had collapsed in a heap. The grass smelled scorched. Downwind, the prairie fire still raged.

They kicked the brush piles apart and let them burn down. As they passed Hampton's wagon, the smells of burnt cornmeal and bacon mixed with those of charred wood and gunpowder. Woodhouse, who had retrieved his silk hat, sniffed expansively. "Ah, back in time for breakfast. Odd way of preparing it, though."

Jake took stock of the camp. Ross was dead. Grinstead was breathing his last. Mrs. Skeffington sat with the old man, talking to him in a low voice, oblivious to the smoke that still swirled around them. Poor Grinstead. He was a retired millwright. His wife was dead, and his children were settled with families of their own; so he had come west to start a new life, to find renewed youth. Now he was choking to death on his own blood in the middle of nowhere.

Pistol shots sounded, one at a time, reverberating across the lightening prairie. Essex and Andrews were killing the wounded animals. Blade was shooting wounded Indians. Molyneaux's $4,000 thoroughbred was put down with a one-cent bullet. A lot of the company's draft animals had been lost in the battle or had run away. There were only enough animals to pull two wagons now.

Jake took Ross's and Nowak's revolver belts and buckled them across his chest, like shoulder holsters. That gave him four pistols. He would not be caught short of ammunition again, as he had been with Yellow Wolf. He put Navy Colts in the shoulder hoslters—Ross's and one of his own. He stuck Nowak's big .44 Colt Dragoon in the holster behind his back. Having the .44 meant carrying different-sized cartridges, but it was worth it. The .44 was a good last-stand gun. A bullet from that would knock down a horse.

Jake walked to Mrs. Skeffington's wagon, coughing from the remnants of the smoke. The red ball of the sun had peeped over the horizon. Jake suddenly felt very tired and very thirsty. His steps faltered, and he wondered if he could go on. Then he saw Harvey Reed leaning against the large rear wheel of the wagon. The boy had his head on his arms. He was sobbing, and Jake knew that Jim Hart had died.

Jake braced himself. He had to go on. He was the captain; he was the Hero of Chapultapec. He placed a hand on Harvey's gray-jacketed shoulder, trying to be of comfort, feeling inadequate.

Harvey looked up. His blue eyes were red-rimmed, and the scaly skin beneath his thin beard was wet. His voice quavered with disbelief. "He was so strong. I thought if anyone could pull through, it would be Jimmy."

"Things don't always work out like we figure," Jake said quietly.

"I've known Jimmy all my life. We grew up together. It's not fair, it's just not fair. He shouldn't have to die."

Fresh tears flowed down the boy's cheeks, leaving little smears of powder and dirt. "First Willinsky, then Novak, now Jimmy. I'm next, aren't I? I'm going to end up in a dirt hole in this godforsaken wilderness, just like the rest of them. I wish I'd never heard of California. I wish I'd never heard of gold."

"Calm down," Jake told him. "We got us a ways to go, and I'm going to need your help."

"Help? What can I do? I can't shoot. I can't ride."

"You can start by helping me with Sloane. We're moving him to another wagon. Come on, now."

Harvey wiped his eyes with his sleeve. He crawled over the tailboard of Mrs. Skeffington's wagon, and he and Jake helped Sloane get out. The photographer's cholera was past; all he needed was rest. He'd be able to sit a horse by late today or tomorrow—if there were any horses left by then.

Hart's death had made one decision easier for Jake. They would abandon this sick-wagon. It reeked of cholera. Lambert's leg was going to be bad enough; there was no sense exposing him to disease as well. They would use Molyneaux's wagon for the wounded and sick. It was the best made, the least likely to break down. That left one more wagon to take—Webb's or the Alabama boys'. Webb would start whining if they left his. Anyway, his was a bit larger than the others. It would hold more food and ammunition, and that quality could prove crucial. Slowness didn't matter anymore; they would all be going slow.

"Ethan," Jake said, "we're leaving your wagon here. You and Culpepper help me and Harvey break it down and make pack saddles for the extra mules. Pile 'em with food and ammunition."

When the task was done, Ethan observed, "We'll never make California on these supplies."

"We can re-outfit in El Paso," Jake said. "First we got to get to Comanche Crossing, though. First we got to get water."

"How far is it to this Comanche Crossing?" asked Harvey.

"I ain't certain. Twenty miles, might be. Might be more.

The Lower Road turns north a bit to come up on it. When we make that turn, we're close."

"You stop there last winter?" Culpepper asked.

"Yeah, but we was coming from the other direction. Country looks different that way." In reality Jake hadn't paid much attention to the country, because he hadn't planned on returning, but he didn't tell them that.

The two wagons were ready. The last bits of personal gear were abandoned, along with sacks of corn and sides of bacon for which there was no longer room, and which were burned to keep them from falling into the Indians' hands. Nowak's violin came out of Webb's wagon. Even to Jake, who knew nothing about music, the violin was exquisitely crafted. Nowak had kept it cleaned and polished, in a velvet-lined walnut case. Jake laid it inside the Alabama wagon, where it would suffer least from the elements. It was unlikely, but maybe somebody would be able to use it someday.

Woodhouse was taking a last look at his carefully preserved specimens. They were the fruits of his trip to America. They represented his last chance professionally, and he was glum as he parted with them—a thrush, a cardinal, an iridescent green jay, many more. He held up his prize, a hawk with two white bands on its tail. "*Falco lagopus,*" he told Jake. "I especially hate to give this one up. Still, there's nothing for it. At least I have my sketches in my saddlebags, though God knows how much longer I'll be able to keep those." He plucked one of the hawk's tail feathers and stuck it in the band of his silk hat.

Culpepper limped up. "How 'bout the dog?" he asked Jake. He nodded his head toward one of Molyneaux's brindle mastiffs. The big dog was lying mournfully by its master's grave, head on its paws. The other mastiff had been killed by an arrow during the battle.

Jake hated making these decisions. He hated having the power of life and death, even if it was over a dog. "We ain't got food nor water, not for a dog that size."

"You're not going to shoot it?" Woodhouse said.

"No, turn him loose. Give him a chance. Maybe the Comanches'll take him in, though probably death's better than the way they treat dogs."

Culpepper shook his head. "You know, I always hated them dogs. Always figured them dogs would end up eatin' me. Now I feel kinda sorry for that one. Life sure is funny, ain't it?"

"Hilarious," Woodhouse said.

Nearby, Cutter's gray terrier Sparky was running back and forth, sniffing the ground. Cutter said, "Leave that one, too?"

Jake hesitated, then nodded.

The sun was well up as the company ate a hurried breakfast of steaks and horsemeat. They buried the dead, and put up four new crosses next to Molyneaux's. There were too few wagons to try to hide the gravesites now. "Put one up for McWilliams, too," Jake said. "Maybe it'll help him, wherever he's gone."

As they walked from the graves, Mrs. Skeffington said to Cutter's widow, "Put your bonnet on, dear. You must have something on your head with this sun."

Mrs. Cutter took the straw bonnet. She still looked dazed, and Jake wondered if she even knew where she was anymore. She hadn't eaten breakfast, and she seemed about ten years older than she had a week ago.

The company formed up. There were two wagons, one pulled by mules, one by oxen. There were thirteen people, four horses, and three pack mules. Their water was almost gone. Food and ammunition were short. The animals were on their last legs, and the people weren't far behind.

Before they set off, Harvey Reed looked at Jake anxiously. "Are we going to make it, Captain Jake? Tell me the truth."

The truth was that they'd probably all be dead this time tomorrow. Should Jake tell them that? Others were looking at him, too—Ethan, Mrs. Skeffington, Culpepper, Essex, Woodhouse, Webb.

Jake made himself grin, as though he hadn't a care in the world. "Sure, we'll make it. I been through worse than this, plenty of times. Hell, in Puebla in Mexico, we was so hungry we was ready to eat each other 'fore the relief column pulled through. We was so thirsty, we was drinking snake piss. Why, I've been in spots so tight . . . ."

He went on, making up tall stories. The men—especially the younger ones—listened to him, wide-eyed. They believed him. They needed to believe. He hated himself for lying, but it made them feel better. "Come on," he said at last. "Let's get out of here."

19

They found McWilliams just after noon.

Jake and Hampton were walking point. They saw the circling buzzards first, then McWilliams. Yellow Wolf's Comanches had left him on the trail, in an open spot where the emigrants were certain to find him. Among other things, the Indians had sliced off the soles of the Ranger's feet, then made him walk, naked, for miles behind their ponies. He had been scalped and staked out facing the sun, with his eyelids cut off. His screams had stopped because they had cut out his tongue.

He was still alive.

Jake's knees sagged. He felt like he had to sit down. He looked next to him. Hampton was unnerved as well. There was a clump of hooves and a jingling of chains as the wagons came up behind them. There was no sign of the Comanches. They could be ahead of the company; they could be behind. They could be fifty miles away.

The emigrants reacted to the sight of McWilliams with shock, revulsion, and oaths. "Oh, good God," muttered Woodhouse. Essex stood breathing heavily, jaw muscles clenched. Blade swore and shook his fist at the empty horizon. Webb sank to his knees in prayer. Mrs. Skeffington wept. Harvey Reed hid his eyes.

Jake stepped forward, reaching behind his back for the big .44. This was his job. It was his fault McWilliams had ended up this way. Jake prayed forgiveness for that mistake and for what he was about to do. His scarred hand throbbed from the fight with Hampton. It hurt to grip the heavy pistol. He was shaking. His teeth chattered, as if he were cold. He tried not to look at McWilliams's burned-out eyes; he tried to ignore the gagging sounds from what used to be McWilliams's throat. He leveled the revolver and put a bullet in the Ranger's brain.

The shot echoed over the wide plain. Relief flooded through Jake, followed by self-disgust. He looked anywhere but at the . . . the *thing* at his feet. He'd never killed a man in cold blood. He never wanted to do it again.

He struggled to stay upright. It was his fault. His fault. He should be the one staked out here, not McWilliams. He wished he could have changed places with him. No—no, he didn't. He wasn't man enough to wish something like that. He wasn't man enough to take full responsibility for his actions.

Essex came up beside him. He spoke quietly, "McWilliams's revenge, Yellow Wolf's revenge. Where does it get them? The poor fellow finished up just like his family." He looked at Jake and nodded. "You did the right thing."

"Yeah," Jake said, and his voice croaked. "Let's bury him and keep moving."

It was the hottest day yet, as if Nature itself conspired against the company. The landscape never changed, endless desert with distant mountains on both sides. The country was a series of undulations, of breaks and dry streambeds. The trail went constantly up and down, wearing on men and beasts.

The animals had been dying since mid-morning. They sank to their knees, and no amount of prodding could make them rise again. The first to go had been a horse. Blade and Hampton had stood the dead animal upright, saddled him, and pointed him west. The company had laughed at this macabre signpost, the laughter of the damned. "Do the same to me when I go," Woodhouse had cracked.

The discovery of McWilliams took the starch out of them, though. It was as if they were ready to give up now, to get it over with and die. Jake moved up and down the line, exhorting them, not because he wanted to, but because that was what they expected of him. "Come on, men, keep moving. We'll make it. Come on, Harvey, don't quit now. What would Jim Hart say? Think of all that gold waiting for you in California. Think of the water waiting at Comanche Crossing."

Lambert felt the pain now. He cried out each time the wagon jolted over a rock, each time it rolled down a hillock or climbed a ravine. Jake had cleaned the boy's wound, picking pieces of bone and cloth from the bloody puncture. The boy needed a surgeon, though. The best they could do was to try to keep him alive until he got to one. In a way he was lucky. The wound was just above the knee. That gave the infection a long way to spread before it was fatal. Probably he would lose his leg at the hip. Jake had heard of men amputating limbs with bowie knives, but he was not good enough to do that. He didn't have the guts. There was nothing to ease the blond boy's agony. The brandy was all gone, and Jake cursed himself for tossing off half a bottle so cavalierly the day he was elected captain of the train.

Mrs. Skeffington sat with Lambert, holding his big hand, talking to him and comforting him as best she could. She hadn't slept in two days. Her eyes sagged, and sometimes she dozed off as she talked. Her gray hair was bedraggled. She still wore the filth-splattered dress, though she'd tried to brush it clean.

The pace of the march slowed. Tongues hung out. Eyes were slits in swollen, blistered faces. Throats burned so badly from thirst that it was hard to breathe. Some of the men's boots had worn out, and they wrapped their feet in moccasins made from the green hide of a slaughtered ox. Their feet were cut and bleeding from sharp rocks and prickly pear cactus.

"Keep going, men. Keep going," Jake said. "See them two mountains over there? The big ones? On the way out from California, the boys called them the 'Mexican Tits.' The turn north's right near here.'' There *had* been two mountains, and the dragoons *had* called them ''Mexican Tits,'' but Jake did not remember if it was those two or not. He was just saying something to keep the company moving, to make them think there was a reason for going on.

Mrs. Cutter walked along in a daze. ''Where's your bonnet?'' Jake asked her.

The widowed pioneer woman looked around, confused. ''I . . . I don't know.''

Jake cut some canvas from Webb's wagon cover. He wrapped it around Mrs. Cutter's head, like a turban. ''There,'' he said. It was the best he could do.

She didn't thank him. She didn't say anything. Her eyes were strange, as if she saw something in the distance that was visible to no one else. Now and then she grinned crazily. But she kept moving.

Cutter's gray terrier Sparky trotted along with the column. Jake shooed the dog away, but he kept coming back. Sparky's paws were rubbed raw, then cut open on the hot sand and rocks. He stopped and looked at Jake, grinning and panting. He moved on a few steps, then stopped again. He lay down, still grinning, fixing Jake with his brown eyes. Jake sighed. He scooped up the little dog and put him in Mrs. Skeffington's wagon, where he lay on his side and promptly fell asleep.

The sun burned down harder, a living force. The men had a few drops of stale coffee left in their canteens, drops they hoarded like liquid gold. The animals had nothing. One by one, the beasts died. As Mrs. Skeffington's mules went down, they were replaced by the pack mules, and the packs were abandoned. The food was burned or scattered to the wind, and the ammunition was blown up with a crude fuse.

The emigrants faced starvation now, as well as thirst. ''We'll stay alive as long as we can eat the animals and drink their blood,'' Ethan said, as they cut another dead mule from its traces. ''But when they're gone, what then?''

''Then you'll do as Captain Moran tells you,'' Mrs. Skeffington said confidently. Nearby, Essex nodded, and Jake wanted to scream. Why did they put it all on him?

''Keep your formation, there,'' Jake called. ''Keep your eyes peeled.'' They must make some pretense at organization. Maybe that way the emigrants wouldn't notice how bad things had gotten; maybe they could be persuaded that the situation was still manageable. Yes, that was the word for it: ''manageable.'' Jake let the word roll around on his tongue, and he realized that he was saying it aloud. Hampton was staring at him with his one good eye, looking at him like he'd gone mad. Maybe he had gone mad. He didn't know. He wanted to laugh, then he stopped himself. ''Manageable.'' This was nothing if not manageable. Then he did laugh, and he kept walking.

Webb's wagon struggled along with a jury-rigged yoke of three oxen. Their teamster, Blade, used every trick he knew to keep them moving. Then another ox died. The remaining two animals gave their hearts to the task, with Blade's whip cracking over their heads, but the heavy wagon was too much for them. Another ox lay down, never to rise again.

''That's the end of that,'' Jake said. ''Cut this last one loose and we'll have him for supper.''

Webb looked terrified. ''I can't leave my wagon, Captain.''

''Well, you sure as hell ain't goin' to pull it yourself, and that's the only alternative.''

''We can take the mules from Mrs. Skeffington's wagon. We can put the sick men in mine.''

''Sure, we could. But why should we?''

''My wagon's better made. It's got more chance of getting through. Let me show you the special contruction inside.''

''Webb, we ain't got time for—''

"Please, it will only take a minute."

"Oh, all right. Anything to keep you quiet." Jake raised his voice to the company. "We'll take a break here."

The exhausted men traded glances as Jake climbed over the tailboard of Webb's wagon, followed by the flaxen-haired newspaperman.

The wagon was crammed with sacks of food, with boxes of cartridges, with blankets. It was stifling under the canvas. Webb glanced nervously to the front and rear, as if he were afraid of someone looking in. He took off his glasses and wiped the sweat from his thin eyebrows. He put the glasses back on and rapped the side of the wagon box. "Solid maple, Captain. The frame is ash, hand picked. The tongue and hounds are the finest hickory."

"Great," Jake said, "but—"

Webb lowered his voice. "And look at this floor." He shifted a 100-pound sack, straining. He pried a finger under a knot in one of the floorboards. Several of the boards came up together, revealing a compartment underneath, about a foot deep, packed with wooden shavings.

Jake's eyes narrowed. Webb glanced around again, then he swept aside some of the shavings, to uncover a bulging sack. "Look closer," he whispered.

With one hand, Jake picked up the sack. It was unusually heavy for its size, filled with something metallic that could only be coins. Jake opened the drawstring. The sack was full of ten-dollar gold eagles.

Jake hefted the sack thoughtfully. He looked around. "The whole wagon?"

Webb nodded. No wonder the wagon had been so slow.

"How much?" Jake said.

"Fifty thousand dollars."

Jake's eyes opened wide. He whistled low. "What for?"

Webb leaned in close. Sweat rolled down his face and into his dirty beard. His breath smelled foul. "Have you ever heard of the Knights of the Golden Circle, Captain?"

Jake shook his head.

"It's an organization of wealthy, influential Southrons. They're thoughtful men, as well. They've seen the expansion of the North. They know our Southron way of life is doomed unless we expand also. California's entrance to the Union has upset the balance between slave states and free. President Pierce has promised that the South shall have Cuba, but we cannot wait. It looks as though Kansas may be organized as a free state, putting us two down."

Jake sat back on his haunches. It seemed hotter than ever in the wagon. A fly buzzed. Webb's eyes were alight, displaying a craftiness, a shrewdness, that Jake had never noticed before. "This money is to buy arms and recruit men for an expedition to Nicaragua."

Jake's eyes opened wide for a second time. "Nicaragua!"

"It's the ideal choice. Nicaragua sits astride the route from the Atlantic to the Pacific. The transit tolls alone are enough to finance a government. In addition, the land is unusually fertile."

"It's also full of malaria, cholera, and *vomito negro*," Jake said. "You know why they call it *vomito negro*? I do. I been in that part of the world."

"Slaves are used to that climate."

Jake shook his head. "Slavery's dead, Webb. It's got ten years, fifteen at the outside. You're living a dream."

He started to rise, but Webb grasped his arm with the sudden strength of passion. "No dream, sir. We plan to use the annexation of Nicaragua as a springboard to Southern independence. It will open the entire Caribbean Basin for our expansion. Unfettered from Northern domination, we will establish an empire of states based on slavery and agriculture, the best economic system yet devised by man. And the Southern Confederacy, not the United States, will become the most powerful nation in the hemisphere."

Jake looked at him. He'd underestimated the man. He smiled wryly. "So the printing press was just a cover. You're really some kind of secret agent."

"An agent for us, Captain. For our people. War is coming, and the sooner the better. The Yankees outnumber us, their industry grows faster than ours. Still, we can beat them if we fight them now. A few years from now . . . who knows? The conquest of Nicaragua can precipitate such a war."

Webb leaned in closer. There was urgency in his voice. "This wagon must get through. I will give you a thousand dollars and a commission as major in our enterprise. You'll receive five hundred acres of land in Nicaragua, tax free, plus a salary. We need men like you, Captain. The men who marched with Scott and Taylor. The men who took Chapultapec. What do you say? Will you join us?"

Jake took off his hat and turned it idly in his hands. "Webb, right now I'm more interested in saving my life than saving your money. And as for your proposition . . . frankly, I don't think you got a chance in hell. You sure ain't got me."

Jake put his hat back on. He returned the sack full of money to the secret compartment and lowered the floorboards. He heard the scrape of leather, then a loud, metallic click. He turned and found himself looking down the octagonal barrel of Webb's Navy Colt.

"The wagon goes through, Captain."

"Or what?" said Jake.

"Or I'll kill you."

The heat seemed to grow even more intense. A large bead of sweat rolled down Webb's nose and dropped off. Jake's guts churned with fear. Webb's pistol had a quick trigger; one slip of a nervous finger would blast Jake into eternity.

Jake willed himself to look calm. He willed himself to look confident. "You ain't goin' to kill me."

"Why not?"

"Because if you do, you'll have to explain it to them out there. You'll have to tell them about the money. What do you think Hampton's going to do when he finds out you got fifty thousand dollars in here? Think he'll let you keep it? Think he'll let you live?"

Webb licked his lips. He took a tighter grip on the revolver.

" 'Sides," Jake said, "shoot me and you won't find Comanche Crossing. You'll die of thirst." That wasn't true. This trail would lead them right to the water hole, but Jake counted on a man in Webb's agitated condition not to think of that.

"Make you a deal," Jake went on. "Put away that cannon, and I won't tell about the money. That way, you got a chance of someday coming back for it."

"What about you?" Webb said suspiciously.

"I ain't comin' after it. Nothing could get me to come through this country again."

The revolver barrel wavered. Slowly the hammer lowered.

Webb put the weapon down, and Jake let out his breath with relief. The fight had gone out of Webb; he seemed suddenly resigned. "There's no way we can take the wagon?"

Jake shook his head. "It's too heavy."

The bespectacled secret agent slumped against the side of the wagon box. He looked devastated. "I never expected to meet defeat on this mission. So many were counting on me. I'm a failure."

"It ain't your fault," Jake said. He clapped Webb's shoulder, "Come on. We have to go."

Jake's remark did little to restore Webb's confidence. The erstwhile newspaperman looked distinctly crestfallen as he climbed out of the wagon behind Jake.

The others were watching them, curious. "What was that about?" Blade asked.

Jake sidestepped the question. "We're leaving Webb's wagon. I persuaded him. Unyoke this last ox."

"Shall we transfer some cornmeal to Mrs. Skeffington's wagon?" asked Essex.

"No, the mules can't pull no more weight. We'll have to make do with what we have."

The company marched away, leaving Webb's wagon, leaving the fifty thousand dollars. Maybe Webb would be back for it someday. Maybe not. Right now there were more important things to worry about.

The last ox died soon after. They cut it up and drank its blood. They were getting used to animal blood. They staggered on. The trail did not turn north. Jake wondered if somehow he'd missed the turn. He wondered if they were marching to their deaths, and he decided that they probably were.

When the emigrants made camp that evening, Jake called them together. They sat wearily or reclined around the one small fire. With their beards and dirt, their wounds and tattered clothes, the emigrants looked more savage than the Indians. They stared at Jake with dull eyes, save for Mrs. Cutter, whose vision was focused somewhere in the distance—or was it in the past?

"I need a volunteer," Jake told them, "to ride for help. The Army's building a fort south of here, called Davis. They've got a couple companies of Mounted Rifles there."

"Christ save us all," moaned Essex, who shared the Navy's traditional contempt for the Army. "That means infantry riding mules. The only way they'll hurt the Comanches is if the Indians laugh themselves to death."

A few of the men chuckled. Mrs. Skeffington laughed, too. She knew the Army too well not to. Jake went on, "With luck, there'll be a company of Texas Militia as well. Bring them if you can. At least they have horses. Have them bring extra water, food, and a doctor if there is one. Now, who'll go?"

Essex raised his hand. So did Hampton. So did Blade and Woodhouse, Culpepper and Andrews. Brave men, braver than Jake.

Jake had already decided whom he wanted. "Culpepper," he said.

"The nigger?" Ethan said.

"He won't bring help," Hampton said. "Not for us. He'll run to Mexico."

"Damn you for a nigra lover, Moran," swore the embittered Webb. "I should have known."

Jake remained calm. "I got two reasons. First, Culpepper's a good rider. Second, he's a god-awful shot, and we need everybody that's handy with weapons here."

Culpepper laughed, unusual for him. "Where I comes from, they don't much fancy teachin' black folks how to shoot."

Culpepper took the best of the three remaining horses, a grulla with black ear tips and a black mane. He traveled light, with a *morral* of parched corn and one revolver. Jake had everyone give him some coffee-water, sharing their last drops until he had nearly a full canteen.

"Goddamn it," Hampton said. "Now we die of thirst to save this nigger's black hide." Others grumbled agreement.

When it was fully dark, before the quarter moon had risen, Culpepper mounted. "Ride south till you hit the Rio Grande," Jake told him, "then east. You should make it in about two days, a day and a half if you travel quick. Maybe you'll run into one of their patrols before you reach the fort. Have them come to Comanche Crossing. For God's sake, make them hurry."

Culpepper nodded. He gathered the reins.

"Good luck," Jake said.

"Yeah," said the black man. He wheeled the horse and was quickly lost in the darkness. The cantering hoofbeats receded into the night.

"That's the last you'll see of your pet coon," Webb told Jake.

"Amen," Blade said, shaking his head.

"He'll be back," Essex said confidently.

"Of course he will," added Mrs. Skeffington.

The emigrants listened, straining their ears. For a long

time they heard nothing, just the usual night sounds. Then there came the distant report of a pistol. It was followed by a ragged volley of shots, then a single carbine shot. Then silence.

The emigrants hung their heads.

20

They left camp well before dawn, while the air was still cool. Few of them had gotten much sleep. One of the horses was nearly dead, and they slaughtered it for breakfast, but it was hard to chew the broiled meat with nothing to wash it down. The animals did not eat at all; their mouths were too dry. This would be the company's last day without water. They would find water today, or they would die.

They moved slowly. They were tired and thirsty and weakened by dysentery. Their heads spun with pain; their skins were blistered. Their eyes hurt from weeks of exposure to the sun, and some of them were going blind. Their gums were bleeding; now and again they bent over from the pain of stomach cramps.

In the east, the sky lightened. The sun made its fiery entrance on stage. It grew hot. Dust rose in choking clouds.

"Look at this," Woodhouse said. "I mean, it's May. There should be flowers, green grass. Rustics singing in the fields." He shook his head. "And people back in England complain when it rains."

Beside him, Dan Essex hobbled on blistered feet. "Now I know why I joined the Navy. You don't have to walk."

The animals were red-eyed. Their tongues drooped. One of the mules died almost immediately. Not long after, the company's last horse went to its knees, trembling, frothing. It fell over, its emaciated chest rising and falling. The emigrants marched past the animal, hardly sparing it a glance.

Another mule gave out. That left two mules, and they couldn't pull the sick-wagon—not in their condition.

"Looks like the end of the road for the wagon," Jake said.

Some of the emigrants took their few remaining possessions—food, ammunition, money, a hackberry toothbrush, a razor, an extra pair of socks, a length of rope perhaps, a tin drinking cup and bowl, a frying pan—from the wagon and wrapped them in their blankets. They tied the ends of the blankets with twine and slung them across their shoulders. Others carried their goods in sacks or bundles. Some carried food in leather pails.

Jake wanted to make a travois for Lambert, like the Indians used. There were no trees for the poles, however. They had to use the wagon tongue and reach pole, and these were shorter than Jake would have liked. The wounded man's head would be dangerously close to the mule's hind legs. "It's all right," Lambert said, white-faced with the pain of his shattered leg but still grinning. "I been kicked by better mules than this." They shaped the poles with their last ax, and they bound canvas from the wagon to them. Sloane rode the other mule. Neither animal had much left in him.

The company trudged along, leaving bloody footprints in the sand. Andrews held the bridle of Lambert's mule. Essex walked alongside the other mule, holding Sloane on. Sparky the terrier limped at Jake's heels. The little party was lost in the immensity of the prairie. They crawled across the vastness like wayward ants. For all man's belief in being favored by God, they counted for nothing in this world. They could vanish and never be missed. Their loss would go unnoticed, as their presence had been, by this great primordial land.

Jake stumbled in and out of reality. He went through periods when he did not know what was happening. Time ceased to exist. The flaming ball of the sun hung suspended overhead, a living weight on his shoulders, burning a hole through his brain. The crossed revolvers dangled heavily from his chest; the Sharps rifle was heavy, too. Ammunition was crammed in his blanket roll. He didn't like carrying so much weaponry, but it was necessary. He wished he could have carried more.

"Look!" cried Harvey Reed suddenly, pointing. "Look there!"

"Oh, my God, it's water!" rasped Ethan.

"A lake!" Blade said. "We're saved, boys!"

To the south of them, the land fell away in a broad plain. At the end of the plain, shummering through the heat, was a wide blue lake, surrounded by a fringe of trees.

"I've never seen anything so beautiful," Webb said, laughing with joy.

Harvey turned to Jake. "Is it Comanche Crossing?"

Jake answered grimly, "It's a mirage. It ain't really there."

Several of the men began talking at once. " 'Course it's there. We can see it. What do you mean it's not there?" The lake looked so real you could almost swim in it.

"I said it ain't there," Jake told them savagely. "There ain't no lakes in the middle of the desert."

Mrs. Skeffington spoke through cracked lips. "I'm afraid Captain Moran is right. My husband has often described such phenomena to me."

Essex agreed. "We have something similar at sea. On becalmed days in the tropics, you sometimes see phantom ships, or land where there is none."

Shoulders sagged. There was an audible sigh of disappointment.

"Come on," Jake said. "Keep moving. It don't do us no good to stand here."

Reluctantly, the company marched on. Some of the men turned for a last look at the blue lake. Mrs. Cutter stood staring, shading her turbaned eyes with her hand. She was taking it harder than the rest. "Come along, ma'am,"

Woodhouse said, bringing up the rear. "You don't want to fall behind."

"What?" she said. "Oh, yes. I'll be right there."

Woodhouse passed on.

The emigrants shuffled along. Step by step, and each step the same, taking them nowhere. The trail made no turn north. They had missed Comanche Crossing. Jake had missed it. His stupidity was going to get them all killed, just as he had known it would from the day they had elected him captain. He supposed it didn't matter, now. The seed was sown, it remained only to reap the terrible—

"Where is Mrs. Cutter?" Mrs. Skeffington said. Jake turned. Mrs. Skeffington was staring back down the trail. Cutter's widow was nowhere to be seen.

The others stopped as well. "She was looking at that mirage," Woodhouse said. "I assumed she was right behind us."

How long had that been? Half an hour? Someone had to go back for her. "Help me get Sloane off this mule," Jake said to Essex.

They assisted Sloane in dismounting. Jake got on the mule and started back along the trail, kicking the reluctant animal into a semblance of speed. He came to the place where they had seen the mirage, and he scanned the horizon. Mrs. Cutter was nowhere in sight. He found her footprints, heading south, as he had known they would be. He kicked the mule after her. The tracks wandered from side to side, as if their maker had been staggering.

He found Mrs. Cutter at the foot of a small break. Her body was lying face down in a fall of gravel. Her right hand was outstretched. Her thin, worn fingers were dug into the sand, as if with her last breath she had been grasping for something.

Jake hung his head.

When Jake returned to the company, he said nothing. He just shook his head and helped Essex get Sloane back on the tired mule.

The emigrants kept going. There was no talking. They withdrew into themselves, conserving themselves for the fight against the sun. They passed more abandoned wagons, more bones of animals. They discarded things—a blanket here, a coat there. Webb threw away the company log. Men stumbled, got up, and kept going.

Suddenly the quiet was split by a loud rattle, followed by a hiss. Jake had an impression of a coiled body, brownish green and yellow, glistening as it struck. Lambert's mule cried out and leaped into the air, breaking Ethan's grip on the reins. The bitten animal began plunging and kicking. Lambert's head thudded sickeningly with each kick. He had been tied on the travois, so that he would not fall off.

"Son of a bitch!" yelled Ethan.

The poisoned animal began running. The travois bounced crazily in its wake. The emigrants ran after it. Jake forced his tired body into the pursuit.

The mule dodged this way and that, maddened by the pain of the snakebite. The emigrants yelled and waved their hands, lunging for the reins, missing and falling in the dust. The travois bounced over rocks. One tie broke, but still it hung on. Finally the other tie loosened. The mule gave a mighty buck to rid itself of its encumbrance, sending the travois spilling down the side of an arroyo.

As the mule ran off to its death, Jake and Ethan and Essex came to the edge of the arroyo. The big farm boy Lambert lay halfway down the arroyo's side with his wounded leg bent behind him. The three men slid down, scattering stones in their path. Blood was coming from Lambert's ears, trickling into his blond beard.

"Skull's broke," Jake said.

"Is he breathing?" Essex asked.

Jake put his ear to the boy's mouth, then to his chest. "Little bit."

Ethan brushed his long dark hair out of his eyes. He

rounded on Jake. "So what are you going to do? Put a bullet in him? Same as you done to the Ranger?"

"No, son," Jake said quietly. "No bullet."

By some miracle, Lambert's leg was unbroken. Jake took off his black bandana and used it as a tourniquet to stop the fresh bleeding. Then the three men, with the aid of Woodhouse, who had just clambered down the arroyo, lifted Lambert onto the travois.

They picked up the travois, using it as a stretcher, and started up the hill. They climbed carefully, each man holding a pole end, trying not to jar the injured boy too much. There was pink froth at his lips; he must have sustained internal injuries as well. Ethan pleaded with his boyhood friend tearfully, "Don't die on me, George. Keep going. We got us gold to dig, remember?"

Lambert's eyelids fluttered.

"Come on, partner. Hang in there now. You can do it."

Ethan was still talking as they carried Lambert back to the rest of the company. They laid down the travois, and Jake listened for the boy's breath again. He stopped and pressed his ear closer to Lambert's mouth. He wet a finger and held it to the boy's lips.

Ethan said, "Is he . . . is he . . . ?"

Jake nodded.

"Oh, no!" The words came from within, an atavistic howl. Ethan clenched his fists helplessly and pressed them against his forehead, crying. "He only come on this trip because of me. He didn't want to leave his folks, but I talked him into it. I told him what a high time we'd have."

The men scraped out a shallow grave with their knives, and they laid Lambert's body on it.

"Better keep the stretcher," Jake said.

Essex glanced at Sloane. "For him?"

Jake nodded again.

They moved out. Sloane's mule—the one Jake had ridden hard to find Mrs. Cutter—was finished. They were squeezing the last steps from it. Finally it could go no further. Its legs trembled; its swollen tongue hung out. Its eyes were bulging; its chest heaved. It fell to its haunches, with its front legs splayed.

Sloane stepped awkwardly from the saddle. He stood on weak legs. His face was sunken, skeletal.

"Can you walk?" asked Jake.

"Sure," Sloane gasped bravely. "I'm fine. Just a little thirsty."

Sloane put his arms around Essex's shoulders, and the company started off again. They had not gone far before Sloane's feet were dragging. His toes dug lines in the dirt. Essex looked at Jake and shook his head.

Jake halted the company. He brought the stretcher back. "Come on, Frank." As Sloane lay on the stretcher, Jake swore at the girl who had jilted the photographer, whose fickle attentions had condemned the quiet, inoffensive young man to this.

"I'll hold Sparky," Sloane said.

Jake handed him the grateful dog, whose bloody paws left stains on the photographer's shirt. Then Jake and Essex, along with Woodhouse and Harvey Reed, lifted the stretcher, and the company resumed its march. They moved like a procession of dead men. Every effort went into taking one more step. Then one more. And one more after that. The heat increased, wave on wave, beating on them like the surf of an invisible ocean, grinding them down. Buzzards followed them.

Jake heard a noise behind him. He turned. Hampton had collapsed. The men laid down the stretcher, and Jake walked back. He stood over the Carolinian. Hampton raised his head from the dust. His clothes hung loosely on his big frame now. His hat had fallen off, and his hair, which had once been well oiled and combed straight back, was now lank and dirty and hung every which way. With his heavy beard, he didn't look like the same man. Jake hated Hampton. He wanted to leave him here. He wanted Hampton's brains to fry in the sun. Jake was a "hero," though; and heroes couldn't act that way.

"Get up, Hampton."

Hampton fixed Jake with his good eye. There was a trapped, animal-like brightness to his gaze.

"Get up!"

"Why? What difference does it make? We're dead whether we make water or not. Why go on?"

"We go on because we have to. That's what makes us men." Jake kicked Hampton's thigh. "Now get your fat ass up and keep moving."

"Oh, leave me be, will you."

"You gutless son of a bitch." Jake reached down. With a strength he thought he no longer possessed, he grabbed Hampton's arms and hauled him to his feet. Hampton shook him off angrily, staggering as he did so. The two men looked at one another. Then Jake shoved Hampton forward, and the company shambled on.

They followed the wagon ruts of earlier years. Each man was lost in his private universe, in his private war with the sun. It was some time before Jake dully realized that the sun seemed to have moved in the sky. The fitful breeze was blowing in his face now, not over his right shoulder.

He looked at Essex. The sailor had realized the same thing. "We've turned north," Essex said.

Jake's heart beat faster, but he refused to let himself hope. He'd been disappointed too many times before.

Almost without knowing it, the emigrants found themselves on a broad path. It was more like a highway than a path, beaten out of the limestone soil over countless years, by thousands upon thousands of horses. It was littered with the ancient bones of animals, with sun-bleached old blankets, with broken cups and weapons and innumerable other bits of rubbish. At one end of this highway lay Mexico; at the other, the Llano Estacado.

"The Comanche war trail," Jake said. Along this trail, parties of Indians rode south in the spring and again in the early fall. In November they returned north along it with their booty. "None of these tracks is fresh, thank God."

The company's pace picked up. Jake was carrying the front of the stretcher. He stumbled, then stopped. He squinted, eyes aching from the sun's glare.

"What is it?" Essex said beside him.

Ahead of them were stands of mesquite. There was a fringe of green grass.

"There's water up there," Jake said. "It's Comanche Crossing."

The party stumbled faster, slinging off blanket rolls, dropping pails and rifles and hats in their haste to reach the water. Sparky jumped out of Sloane's arms and ran with them. Jake and the others laid the stretcher down. "We'll be back in a few minutes," Jake promised Sloane. "With a full canteen."

The company lost all organization. They stumbled in the ruts of the war trail; they stumbled over bleached bones and caught their feet in old clothing stripped from Mexican prisoners. They fell, picked themselves up, and kept running toward the wide sinkhole ahead. They cut themselves, but they did not notice. A low cry rose in their throats, "Water!"

They reached the edge of the hole and plunged down, falling and sliding. Then they scrabbled to a stop on the rocks and stared in disbelief.

The water hole was dry.

21

Blade and Ethan and Harvey Reed sank heavily to the sand, staring with disbelief at the flat dry bottom of the water hole, seamed with drought cracks. Tyler Hampton lay on his back, eyes closed, panting heavily. Webb sat on a rock and hung his head between his knees, crying. Mrs. Skeffington stood upright. She tried hard not to show her emotions. Her sharp chin jutted forward, and her head was thrown back. Dan Essex took off his leather cap and wiped his brow. Woodhouse chuckled and shook his head, as if at the absurdity of it all.

Gradually, they all looked at Jake.

Jake wanted to give up. He wanted to lie down and die. He would have done it, if not for the others. He saw their trusting faces, waiting for his command. With a sickening jolt, it struck him that these people believed the only reason they had made it this far was because of him. It was their faith in him that had enabled them to keep going, even the ones who disliked him. They thought he was a hero leading them to salvation, instead of a coward leading them to their deaths. He hated himself more than ever for going along with the deception. He wanted to throttle them. He wanted to yell at them, "It's not me that did it. It's you. I'm just something you invented." It was too late for that, though. He had to act.

He looked around. The water hole was roughly oval in shape, maybe fifty yards by thirty, with rocks and weeds clustered on its sides. The mesquite flourished nearby, and grass, so there must have been water here some time this year. Sparky limped back and forth at the bottom of the hole, fretting and pawing the hot sand.

Jake pulled his bowie knife from its sheath. "Dig!" he ordered. "All of you. I don't care what you use, but dig!"

He stumbled to the bottom of the hole. Wearily, the emigrants followed. They went to their knees. They began chopping the hard-baked earth with their knives, scraping it out with their hands, making animal noises of pain and thirst. Sloane was brought to the hole on his stretcher. His little porkpie hat was tilted over his eyes. He was either asleep or in a coma; Jake couldn't tell which.

They kept digging. The sun beat down, burning them, mocking their feeble efforts. Webb fell over, exhausted. For a long time nothing came from the deepening hole but sand. Then, almost imperceptibly, the sand turned dark.

They dug harder, feverish with anticipation now. The dark sand turned to mud. The mud began oozing water. An inarticulate cry rose from the emigrants' throats. They crammed handfuls of the wet mud into their mouths, sucking out the precious liquid, spitting the leftover grit to the ground.

"Keep digging," Jake said. "Don't stop now."

They worked with renewed energy. They reached water. The water was cool and delicious beyond description, after the days of thirst and the awful taste of the stale coffee. The emigrants crowded around the hole, scooping the water with their hands, with tin cups, luxuriating in it. The dog lapped the water alongside them, but they didn't notice.

Jake half filled a cup and carried it to Sloane. "Here, Frank." He lifted Sloane's hat and stopped. The photographer's eyes were closed. There was a gentle smile on his lips, but the lips had gone cold.

"Sloane's dead," Jake announced, standing upright.

Woodhouse shook his head. "Poor sod. Come all this bloody way to die of thirst at a water hole."

"What a waste," said scraggly-bearded Harvey Reed,

the last of the Argonauts. "Frank never wanted to come west. He'd never have been here if it wasn't for that girl."

They carried Sloane's body to the shade of the mesquite, then they returned to the water hole. They dug until they were exhausted, until their muscles burned from the effort. By then they had excavated a fair-sized hole, and they could sit back and wait as water seeped into it, refilling it slowly each time they emptied it.

"Drink slow," Jake told them. "Not too much at first, or you'll bust your guts."

Sated, the company lay around the water hole, thanking God for their deliverance.

"We better start thinking about what to do next," Jake said.

"Can't we stay here?" Webb asked. The secret agent had taken off his glasses. His eyes were unfocused and red from too much sun. Probably he still had ideas about somehow going back for his wagonload of gold.

Jake shook his head. "This water will keep us alive for now, but we don't know when it'll run out. It might be weeks—months, even—before another wagon train passes through here."

"There's Indians to worry about, too," Essex said.

Jake nodded. "Sitting in the middle of the Comanche war trail ain't the safest thing I can think of."

Mrs. Skeffington said, "So what do you propose? That we strike out for El Paso?"

"Don't think we'd make it," Jake said. "It's a long walk to Hueco Tanks, and we can't count on finding water in between. Game might be scarce, too, and we're about out of food."

"What do we do, then?" Hampton said.

"I say, head where we sent Culpepper, to Fort Davis. Those who have money left can buy wagons and animals and provisions there. Those like me, who ain't got a cent . . . well, maybe we can find work. It's our only choice."

"Culpepper didn't make it, though," Blade reminded him.

"That's a chance we got to take."

There were no objections to Jake's plan. He said, "We'll stay here today and rest up, then leave in the morning. We'll strike southeast along the war trail; that'll lead us right to the fort."

The rest of the afternoon passed slowly. Most of the men fell asleep. At sunset, Jake lay at the lip of the water hole, watching the distant northwest mountains glow burnished gold amidst the creeping purple shadows. At the bottom of the hole, a small mesquite fire was burning, and a few of the men who had awakened were roasting pinole.

Jake sipped water from his canteen. He was no longer thirsty, but he wanted to force as much of the liquid as possible into his body before starting the long walk south. Footsteps crunched the stone, and Tyler Hampton lowered himself beside Jake.

The Carolinian looked at the mountains for a moment, then at Jake. His tone was apologetic. "I haven't thanked you for saving me back there."

Jake replied tersely, "I didn't save you. You done the walking, not me."

"But I wouldn't have done it if not for you. I'll hand it to you, Moran. You pulled us through."

"It ain't over yet."

"The worst is. Couple days, and we'll be at Fort Davis."

Hampton fumbled in his torn blue coat. He pulled out a silver flask engraved with his initials. "I was saving it for when we reached California, but this seems like a better time."

He unscrewed the cap and offered the flask to Jake. "No hard feelings," Hampton said, and he grinned. The grin was remarkably infectious, and it took the pain of his whip cuts to keep Jake from grinning back.

Jake took the silver flask. He smelled the pungent odor of bourbon whiskey. He tilted the flask and drank. The whiskey burned his throat, and he choked and coughed. He was unused to liquor these last weeks.

He returned the flask. Hampton laughed and put it to his own lips. "You're a better man than I thought, Moran— Jake. I'm sorry for what's passed between us. Really. My father died when I was a babe, you know, and my mother and I had it pretty rough. She always taught me not to let anything get in my way, and sometimes I overdo it. I'm afraid I have a pretty bad temper. I've worked at controlling it, but obviously I still have a way to go."

Jake tempered his coldness. "Well, I'm sorry for taking the company from you, Hampton. I may not have agreed with everything you done, but I never planned no mutiny."

Hampton regarded Jake closely, as if deciding whether to believe what he had said, then he extended the flask again.

"No, thanks," Jake said. His head buzzed from the little he'd already taken. He'd noticed a disturbing affinity for whiskey in himself. Once he started drinking, it was hard for him to stop. Besides, he knew what the aftereffects of liquor could be tomorrow, with the sun beating on his head. It could kill him. He'd seen it happen in Mexico, when soldiers got drunk and died of exposure to the sun.

"Come on," urged Hampton.

"Better not." In the back of his mind, Jake wondered if Hampton wanted him to get drunk. He wondered if Hampton hoped to make him die from the sun, or if he planned to incapacitate him with liquor and then murder him. After all, he'd tried to kill him before. Jake couldn't be sure if Hampton was drinking himself, or just pretending.

Then Jake cursed himself. The man was sincerely trying to make amends, and Jake was still wary of him. Was he that distrustful of everyone, or was he suspicious because he was afraid that Hampton saw through him? Was he starting to believe his own lies? Was he more interested in upholding a false image of himself than he was in making peace?

The two men talked, while it grew dark. Hampton told stories of growing up in rural poverty, of fighting to get ahead, to make life better for himself and his mother. He had more ambition than Jake ever would—hard times did that to a man. Hampton even joked a little as he talked. He could be charming when he wanted to be. It was a side of Hampton that Jake had never seen, and he was surprised to find himself liking the man.

"Sorry we got off on the wrong foot," Jake said after a while.

"So am I," replied Hampton. He touched his blackened eye and laughed. "Sure you won't have another drink?"

"I'm sure."

"Well, I better get some sleep, then. Good night, Jake."

"Good night . . . Tyler."

Hampton sidled off. Jake watched him disappear into the blackness beyond the firelight. He no longer believed that Hampton would follow through on his threats to kill him. Instead he believed that, amid all this tragedy, he had made a friend.

Just before dawn, Jake left his sentry post and wandered out past the mesquite to relieve himself. The little terrier went with him, ranging far and near, pausing to lift his leg against various bushes. The cool darkness smelled of sweet mesquite pods, of sage and dried grass.

Jake stretched and took a hitch at his wool trousers. Suddenly Sparky growled low. "Oh, no," Jake said, thinking of all the sleepless nights the animal had caused.

The terrier growled again, deep in his throat. Jake listened. He heard a noise. It was a horse's hoof, unshod, dislodging a rock.

Jake knelt and quieted the dog with his hand. Jake's hair was standing on end. He felt like his ears were sticking straight out, they were straining so hard.

The silence was vibrant, electric. He heard another hoof fall. Another, farther off. Metal clinked faintly.

Jake drew one of his Navy Colts and fired twice in the air; the flames and explosions split the darkness. "Come on, boy!" he shouted to Sparky, and he sprinted for the water hole.

"Stand to! Stand to!"

There were confused noises from the water hole, muttering and running and clicking of rifle hammers. Then he was over the edge, falling down the side in the darkness, scraping his leg, struggling to recover and scramble back.

"Douse that fire!" he said in a hoarse whisper. "Where's my rifle?"

Voices came out of the blackness. "What is it? What's going on?"

"Horses out there," Jake said. "A lot of 'em."

"Indians?"

"It sure ain't no traveling circus."

Then men threw themselves beside him, weapons ready. Essex handed Jake his rifle. Sparky was barking crazily.

"Get back to your places," Jake said. "We don't know what side they'll be coming from."

The emigrants spread out and waited nervously. The dog stopped barking. The sky began to lighten, and, as dawn spread across the prairie, the men licked their lips and tightened their grips on their rifles.

Massed before them were the Comanches. At their head, on a white horse, was Yellow Wolf.

22

The Indians were a half mile off. There were even more than before. Dust rose from their milling, stamping horses.

"Looks like Yellow Wolf made himself some good medicine," Tyler Hampton said dryly.

"Too damn good," Jake agreed.

"Look at that fellow with all the feathers," breathed Woodhouse, pointing to a rider they hadn't seen before, whose headdress cascaded down his back. "Wouldn't he make a fine painting, though."

"Must be Kiowa," Jake said. "They ride with the Comanches sometimes. Comanches don't wear feathers in their hair, as a rule."

The important Comanches wore buffalo-horn war helmets. Yellow Wolf, though, was bareheaded, to show his shaved patch of mourning. Jake guessed that the old chief had made some sort of vow not to wear his war helmet again until his son's death was avenged.

Jake said, "They're getting ready to charge. Yellow Wolf's talked them into taking this one all the way. He aims to finish us off. Our only chance is to try to turn them."

"Like a buffalo herd?" Woodhouse said.

"Sort of," Jake said. He wiped a hand across his cracked, bleeding lips. "I want the three best shots together . . . here." He picked a spot opposite the center of the Indians, where the mesquite was thin, where horses could charge through unimpeded. This was where they

171

would come. "Take three rifles each, with two people to load for you. That'll be you, Woody, and Tyler and . . . Dan."

"What about you?" Essex said.

Jake shook his head. "I ain't that good a shot."

"Stop being modest, Jake."

Ethan said, "Yeah, how's about that buck you hit with that long shot a few days back? How's about all them ones you killed by yourself? If that ain't good shooting, I don't know what is."

Jake said, "I mean it. I—"

"Take my place," Essex said, pushing Jake forward. "Hurry."

There was no time to argue. Jake lay at the lip of the water hole, next to Woodhouse and Hampton, cursing. It would serve them right if they were all killed because of their hero's bad shooting.

He laid out his Sharps rifle, another Sharps, and a Springfield carbine. Dan and Mrs. Skeffington were his loaders. "Put them here at my right hand, where I can get them without loading. Everybody else, make sure you have two pistols. When I give the word, open up with them."

Opposite them, Yellow Wolf raised his lance. The Indians yelled and kicked their horses forward.

"Aim at their center!" Jake cried.

He raised the long-ranging Sharps and fired. Next to him, Woodhouse and Hampton did the same. He saw a distant rider fall from his horse. He snatched the second Sharps and fired it. Smoke curled into his eyes and nostrils. Already the Indians were at a full gallop, yelling, waving lances and bows and rifles.

Fresh-loaded rifles were passed forward. Jake grabbed them without looking, firing one after the other. The three men sent bullet after bullet ripping into the Comanche center. Riders and horses went down, but the Comanches kept coming. Sweat poured off Jake's brow into his eyes. He picked up the hot rifles as fast as he could. The other rifles were going off continuously. Jake's hand hurt from the fight with Hampton; it hurt each time he pulled the trigger. He was not used to these other weapons, but there was no time for practice. He fired again, and again.

Closer and closer came the yelling mass of savages. They were splendid, bloodcurdling. Through the powder smoke, Jake saw painted faces and bodies, painted horses. He saw scalps waving from lances and bridles and decorated war shields. Gaps appeared in the Indian center, to be instantly closed. Yellow Wolf was in the lead; it was as if he couldn't be hit. More braves and horses went down. Jake was crying out loud. He was standing with excitement, and his stomach went cold because they weren't going to turn the charge.

The Indians were almost on them. For once they were pressing an attack home. Jake threw down his rifle. "Pistols!" he cried. He drew his revolvers and began firing with both hands, thumbing back the heavy hammers, not aiming. Around him the air erupted with noise as the surviving emigrants fired with him.

Jake blazed into the smoke and dust, into the looming, yelling mass before him. Horses reared; men screamed and toppled. The Kiowa with the feathered bonnet was hit. The Indian center was disappearing. A white horse filled Jake's vision, and he knew he was going to die. Then at the last second the Indians swerved to the left and right, firing arrows and rifles and pistols as they went. Jake had an impression of the man next to him being snatched away, like an unwanted puppet. Something warm and slimy splashed his face and dripped down his beard and chest, and as he drew his other two revolvers, he realized it was someone's brains. A stinging pain in his calf made him spin and fall. He heard someone yelp with pain.

"Spread out!" he yelled, getting back to his feet. "Around the perimeter!"

Men went pounding across the water hole as the Comanches rode past, forming their familiar circle. Picking up his rifle, Jake wiped the stinking mess off his face with his sleeve, and he took a quick look around. Next to him, Webb lay on his back, with his open skull smashed like an egg. Nearby, Tyler Hampton was dazed, fingering a deep gash in his cheek from which blood was flowing. Several of the other men showed slight wounds. Ethan's hat had been shot off. There was a bullet in Jake's calf, but it didn't hurt much.

The emigrants had avoided disaster for the moment, but just for the moment. They were almost out of ammunition. The Comanches withdrew out of range, as they had done so many maddening times before. They milled in the distance, then they galloped up in small groups, shooting arrows and firearms before withdrawing again. The perimeter of the water hole was so long that only one or two of the emigrants had a chance to return the fire at any one time.

Jake reloaded his revolvers. He cleaned the rest of Webb's brains from his face and beard and shirt as best he could. The sun rose high in the sky. It grew hot. The emigrants had to dig for more water, which took men off the firing line and tired them out. Mrs. Skeffington carried the canteens around. It seemed there was just enough water in the hole to keep the party alive. Jake almost wished the water wasn't there. Then they could go ahead and die, instead of prolonging the agony.

There was time for reflection and mounting fear. Each man had a section of the perimeter to cover, and a dwindling number of bullets to cover it with. They fired only if the Comanches came very close. Jake counted his remaining rifle rounds. He saw Essex doing the same. "How many?" Jake said.

"Ten. What about you?"

"Thirteen."

"Not the luckiest number, is it?"

Jake tossed Essex one of the paper-wrapped cartridges. "Here."

Essex put the cartridge in his box. "Thanks. Now we can both have bad luck."

Despite the heat and discomfort of their positions, the emigrants had to stay alert, because they could not tell which of the Indians' feints might prove real. As a group of Indians showered Jake with arrows and withdrew, Jake saw that one of them was wearing a patched gray, military-style jacket. Jake recognized the jacket. It had belonged to Jim Hart. That meant the Comanches had been following the company, digging up the graves, looting the abandoned goods and wagons. Jake was glad he had ordered the food and ammunition destroyed. For once he felt that he had done something right.

The day wore on. The emigrants grew dizzy from the heat and lack of shade. They were weak from prolonged dysentery. There was a little cry and a fall of stones. Ethan had fainted. Blade and Harvey Reed dragged him to the bottom of the hole, where Mrs. Skeffington bathed his face with water.

Jake moved around the perimeter, keeping under cover. The pain in his calf was getting worse. It was sharp, burning. "Come on, men," he said, patting shoulders. "You're doing good. Harvey, don't fall asleep there. Hang on."

"Hang on till what?" Woodhouse said as Jake came by him. "It's useless."

"I know," Jake said in a quiet voice, "but we have to do it."

The Englishman grinned through layers of gunpowder and dirt and sunburn. "Play the game, is that it?"

"Something like that."

Jake passed Webb's body and tried not to look at it. Webb's cracked glasses, lying on the ground beside him, reflected the sunlight in a dozen directions. The secret agent's grandiose schemes for a Southern empire were ended now. The Indians must have found Webb's wagon. Jake wondered if they had discovered the $50,000, and he decided that they probably had. Comanches were thorough scavengers. Probably they would use the money to buy rifles and pistols, to buy bags of cheap arrowheads manufactured in England, or in Pittsburgh or Cincinnatti.

Jake lay against the lip of the water hole once more. The sun baked the smeared remnants of Webb's brains on his face and clothes. The stench was unbearable. He watched the Comanches, who were circling lazily, confidently. How many of them had been hit? He wasn't sure. A dozen or fifteen maybe, during the charge. Two or three since. A good score, but not good enough against these numbers. Jake could see Yellow Wolf in the heat-hazed distance, sitting his white horse, giving orders. Curiously, though Jake hated these Indians, and feared them, and believed they would kill him before the day was over, he felt sorry for them.

The Indians were defending their lands the only way they knew. They hadn't asked the whites to come here. Now they found themselves in a war of extermination, the victors of which were preordained. These bands of nomadic savages must eventually be overwhelmed by the vast population and technological prowess of the United States. Bows and arrows were little use against rifles, six-shooters, and cannon. They were even less use against the lawyer, the banker, and the plow. Jake wondered if Yellow Wolf understood this. He wondered if a proud man like Yellow Wolf knew that his way of life was coming to an end. It might take ten years, it might take fifty, but the outcome was inevitable.

The Indians were coming quite close to the water hole now. They sat their horses in little groups, taunting the emigrants to shoot. "They ain't dumb," Jake said, as he made another round of the positions. "They must figure we're low on ammunition. Save your bullets and keep under cover. If they make a last rush, fire like you got all the cartridges in the world. It ain't much, but maybe it'll make 'em think."

He returned to his position. His calf felt like someone

had stuck a red-hot needle in it. Suddenly he realized that
the sun was setting. Was it possible? Had they survived a
whole day? The day seemed to have flown by; at the same
time it seemed to have lasted forever.

"Look sharp," he called, in a voice so parched that it
seemed to come from someone else. "Sunset's another time
they like to attack."

"I wish you'd find a time they *don't* like to attack,"
Woodhouse shouted back.

Even as the emigrants laughed, the little figures on the
plain coalesced. They formed groups that grew suddenly
large, that came from who knew where. It was the mystery
of the Comanches, their ability to seemingly appear and
disappear at will.

"Here they come!" shouted Blade.

The Comanches began streaming toward the water hole
in long lines. Hooves drummed; dust rose; the air filled
with fiendish cries. The Comanches slanted, circling now,
coming closer and closer with each pass, directing a hail
of arrows and bullets at the defenders, who kept under
cover.

"Fire!" shouted Jake. He raised his head above the rim
of the earth. It was like rising into a maelstrom. Something
hummed by his ear. Arrows and bullets kicked up dust all
around him. An arrow bounced off his crossed revolver
belts.

Jake aimed and fired as fast as he could reload his rifle.
His teeth were bared; he was screaming like a savage himself. He heard shouting and cursing; he smelled the all-too-
familiar powder smoke. His rifle jammed; the breech had
fouled. Why the hell hadn't he cleaned it earlier? Some
frontiersman he was. Feverishly, he took a cartridge, bit
off the end, poured powder down the rifle barrel. He remembered the drill from the Army; it was like he'd never
left. He slid the ramrod from its socket, rammed down the
cartridge paper, and spat the ball on top. Though the barrel
was hot, the ball fit loosely. He tore into his shirt, pulled

out Woodhouse's sketch of himself, ripped off a corner, and rammed it tightly over the ball. He raised the rifle, aimed, and fired. An Indian pony staggered. He repeated the process, tearing another piece of the sketch for a patch. He saw Woodhouse looking at him. "Sorry," he said.

"Quite all right," Woodhouse said between shots. "It's hardly a Rembrandt, you know."

The Indians circled closer to the water hole, working through gaps in the mesquite. Several riderless horses galloped past. There was Yellow Wolf. Jake fired at him for what must have been the hundredth time in the past few days and missed. Maybe the old chief really was protected by the gods. Yellow Wolf drew his bow and loosed an arrow. Jake heard a grunt nearby. He turned and saw Dan Essex bent over, grimacing, with the arrow in his stomach. The ex-sailor sat heavily in the dirt. Jake swore wildly, turned back, and began firing his pistols.

Once again the emigrants' defensive fire proved too heavy for the Indians, and they rode off. They were a good mile away when Jake rose with his last rifle bullet. He was crazy with heat and rage. He aimed at a milling group among whom was Yellow Wolf. He fired. There was a moment's pause, then a distant figure reeled in his saddle, hit by the spent bullet. The rest of the Indians hurriedly galloped off.

"Bravo!" yelled Woodhouse. "Well shot!"

Jake limped over to Essex. In the failing light, the sailor was trying to staunch the flow of blood from around the arrow. Jake knelt awkwardly beside him, wincing from the pain of his own wound.

"How is it?"

"I'll be all right," Essex said. He opened his green eyes wide, as if trying to stay awake. "It was strange. I saw it coming. I saw the feathers, the head, everything. It was like it was happening in slow motion." He coughed. "Not slow enough, unfortunately."

Jake put his hand on his friend's shoulder. It didn't matter. Jake was out of rifle bullets, and he had but a handful of pistol rounds left. The rest of the emigrants were in no better shape. They could not hold off another attack. It was just a matter of time now.

DEAD MAN'S CANYON

Because you're God, Eddie," Joe hissed into a maelstrom of pounding blood. The scar on the gunfigher's cheek was a dark brand. "You would not kill a hundred people just if it was safer, only profitable."

23

As night fell, the emigrants waited for the Comanches and their Kiowa allies to resume the attack. They waited for the rush of moccasins on sand. They waited for an arrow in the throat or an ax in the brain. They waited for shadowy forms to come out of the darkness and kill them.

As the hours wore on, exhaustion overtook them, despite the danger. Jake nodded, then he fell asleep. In a dream, he saw the tortured face of McWilliams. The Ranger's burned-out eyes were staring at him, accusing him.

Jake awoke with a start and a little cry of terror. He was shaking, sweating.

Try as he would to stay awake, his eyes closed again. Again he saw that terrible face. Again he came to, sweating.

He stood and almost cried out from the pain in his calf. That would keep him awake if nothing else would. He made the rounds of the positions. Most of the men were sleeping, too. Thank God for the dog. Jake woke them, whispering to them to stay alert, adding words of false cheer. At the bottom of the hole, he found Essex resting comfortably, with the arrow still in his stomach. The arrow's shaft had been broken, so that only a stub remained. Ethan Andrews was awake. Mrs. Skeffington sat at the Alabaman's side, dozing, with her head on her knees.

Jake knelt beside Ethan. "You feeling better?"

Ethan clutched Jake's sleeve fearfully. In the dark, the boy sounded frightened. "I can't see, Jake. I'm blind."

Jake's stomach went cold. Mrs. Skeffington woke with a jerk of the head. Calmly, she removed the boy's hand from Jake's shirt. She steadied him with a strength that belied her refined manner. "There, there, you'll be all right. It's a temporary condition, I told you. It's caused by the sun's glare off the sand. It happens to my husband's men all the time. They almost always recover."

"Almost?" Ethan said.

The old woman realized that she'd made a mistake. She tried to smooth it over. "I didn't mean . . ."

"Don't worry, Ethan," Jake lied with a glibness he did not feel, "you'll be all right. I've had this myself."

"You have? Really?"

"Sure. It goes away. I swear to you."

Ethan lay back. He smiled, comforted. Jake patted his arm, "Rest easy, now."

Jake returned to his position. He blamed himself for Ethan's blindness. He blamed himself for everything that had gone wrong with the company. He felt sick at heart.

The dog started barking, with an abruptness and ferocity that made the emigrants jump. Jake gripped his revolvers, straining his ears. Between the dog's fits of barking, Jake heard faint noises. There was something out there. Indians, or wild animals? Jake's heart beat faster; his senses were alive. His throat was dry, and not from thirst. He waited.

Dawn found him still waiting, along with the rest of the emigrants. They were worn out; their eyes were sunken. They were certain that the first gray light would show the Indians massed for a final attack; instead, it revealed an empty plain.

The emigrants looked at one another. Hope spread over their weary faces.

Slowly, Jake rose to his feet. "My God, I think they must have—"

Bang! A shot kicked up dirt beside him. Jake dropped below the rim of the water hole, breathing rapidly. *Bang!* The rest of the emigrants lowered their heads, too.

Jake peeked over the rim. There was little to be seen, save for a wisp of smoke drifting from a fold in the brown earth. *Bang!* Another shot sounded from the far side of the hole, near the mesquite.

"They must think we got more bullets than we do," Jake said, crouching back down. "With luck, they're low on arrows and ammunition themselves. Maybe they ain't got enough left for another attack. Looks like they've decided to let the sun and hunger do their work for them. They aim to keep us pinned down till we're too weak to fight anymore."

"What can we do about it?" Hampton said.

"Not a thing, far's I can see, 'cept try and outwait them. It'd be suicide to go out there."

"It's suicide to stay, ain't it?" Blade said.

Jake made no reply.

Sentries were posted. They took an occasional look above the rim of the water hole, making sure never to raise their heads from the same spot twice. They were frequently greeted by rifle fire, though they never saw the enemy. "Lucky Indians aren't good shots," said Harvey Reed, fingering a new bullet hole in his hat. Harvey had gained some pluck. A few days earlier, such a near miss would have left him shaking.

Those emigrants not on watch huddled dispiritedly at the bottom of the water hole, eating breakfast, which was a handful each of dried pinole and parched corn. There was no wood for a fire. The hard corn made their bleeding gums worse. Blade pulled out a tooth, looked at it, then tossed it away. "Good grub," he said.

"Better'n some I've had," Jake noted, trying to sound cheerful. "Coming from California last year, I ate mushed grasshoppers at a Papago Indian village in Arizona. Papagoes think grasshoppers is a delicacy. They'd have considered it real unfriendly if I had refused."

"How'd they taste?" Hampton said.

"Not too bad, once they stopped moving."

There was another shot from above. The emigrants flinched instinctively, even though they were in no danger. Mrs. Skeffington said, "I'll give Yellow Wolf his due. Every time I think things are as bad as they can be, he turns the screws a trifle more."

Jake nodded. "Probably the main bunch of Comanches has their base camp at some spring in the mountains. No doubt they're up there relaxing, sending relays of men to keep us pinned down. They're going to wait till they can just ride in and do what they want without any resistance from us—which shouldn't be too much longer."

Mrs. Skeffington had rubbed mesquite gum on Ethan's inflamed eyes, then wrapped them with a wet bandana. The young man was fidgety; he couldn't wait for the bandana to come off.

Dan Essex was awake, and Jake moved beside him. "Hurt much?"

"Not much," Essex said, but his gritted teeth belied that statement. The arrowhead was in too deep to be cut out. If the head was made of barbed flint, it would tear Dan's guts apart to pull it out. If it was made from thin scrap metal, it would bend or break inside Dan's body if they tried to push it through. A real frontiersman like Israel Combs might have been able to get the arrowhead out. Jake could not. They could only hope to get Essex to a doctor, and Jake knew there was no chance of that happening.

They finished eating and returned to their positions. The sun rose above the lip of the water hole, and the long day's ordeal began. Jake looked out. During the night, the Comanches had managed to spirit away the bodies of all their dead except for a few right at the edge of the water hole. That accounted for the noises they had heard. The dead horses were there, too. One horse was still alive, kicking and thrashing and making pitiful noises. He was in a dip of ground where the emigrants could not get a shot at him to put him out of his misery. With this heat, the bodies of men and animals were already beginning to smell. They were crawling with maggots and bottle flies, who were gorging themselves on this unexpected feast. Soon the corpses would start to swell. They would swell until they burst, spewing decayed flesh and corruption. But by that time, the emigrants would be dead themselves.

Jake limped over and tapped Hampton. "Come on. Help me get Webb's body out of here."

Hampton followed. The two men grasped the Southern agent's body and pushed it over the lip of the water hole. They scrambled out, carried the body a few paces, and rolled it away from the hole. Shots rang out; bullets kicked around them, and they dived back under cover.

Wincing from the pain in his leg, Jake looked over at his new friend and grinned. "Still think you can ride through the Indian nations with fifty men?"

Hampton's dark brows came together. He hated admitting that he was wrong. "You might need a few more than fifty," he said at last.

The hot day wore on. Hampton dozed, or tried to. The intermittent gunfire was just enough to keep everyone awake, as it was intended to be. Woodhouse and Blade retreated into their own thoughts. Harvey Reed prayed. Mrs. Skeffington nursed Ethan and Dan Essex. The malevolent sun was boiling Jake's brains inside his skull. His eyes were heavy with lack of sleep. He wanted to close them, but he was afraid. He could not forget last night. He would rather face the Comanches than see McWilliams's mutilated face again.

The men took turns digging for water and refilling the canteens. Just after noon, Jake found himself paired in this duty with Woodhouse, scooping out the mud with their hands, piling it near the ever deepening hole.

Jake was panting from the heat as he worked. "You've surprised me, Woody. When the trouble started, I thought you'd be one of the first to go. I never thought you'd make it this far."

Woodhouse raised a slender eyebrow. "Never thought

I'd made it this far myself, actually. Wouldn't give odds on making it much farther, though.''

The two men sat back and watched water seep into the hole. Woodhouse's silk hat was much battered now, filthy with dirt and sweat. It gave him a raffish look. Lying beside him was the wine-colored coat, and Jake noticed a rectangular bulge in the coat's pocket. "That ain't a book you got in there, is it?"

"Yes, it's *David Copperfield*. Dickens."

Jake was incredulous. "Everything we threw away, and you saved a *book*?"

Woodhouse looked like he considered the action perfectly normal. "I haven't finished reading it."

Jake lowered a canteen into the water. "I loved books when I was a kid. I always wanted to go to school. I wanted to be a teacher or some such. Never had the chance where I come from, though. Reckon it was silly even to think about it." He took out the canteen and capped it. "What are you going to do if we get out of this?"

"Not much chance of that."

"Pretend."

Woodhouse rubbed an earlobe between thumb and forefinger, scrunching up his eyes thoughtfully. "Well, without my specimens, it's doubtful I could produce the paintings for my book. If I were younger and had money, I'd probably purchase a commission in the Army and go off to fight the Russians. As it is, I expect I'll mine for gold in California, like everyone else. What about you?"

"Ain't really thought about it," Jake said. "But I'll guarantee you one thing. It won't involve Indians, nor guns, nor danger. Safety and comfort, them's my watchwords from now on."

Woodhouse grinned. He obviously didn't believe a word of what Jake said.

Jake distributed the full canteens and hobbled back to his position. The pain in his calf was so intense that he could no longer stand it. The bullet didn't feel like it was in deep, and he decided to try to cut it out. He'd already sliced away the top of his boot, to relieve the pressure. Now he took his bowie knife and cut away the ragged wool of his trouser leg. He took his bandana and made a tourniquet for the lower leg, to control the bleeding. From his blanket roll he got his razor. He struck a sulphur match and ran the flame along the razor blade. He'd seen a doctor do that once, though he didn't know the reason for it. When he was done, he grit his teeth. Trying to keep his hand from shaking, he made an incision in the filthy leg, just above the bullet's puckered entry wound. It didn't hurt as much as he'd expected; either that or his leg was going numb. He sliced downward. Amazing how white the flesh was inside. Then little red dots sprang up everywhere, and the blood started flowing. As he cut, he probed downward gently, and when he struck the ball he knew it—he almost shot into the air with the pain. Steadying himself, he worked the razor around the ball. He gave a push, and the lead ball popped out in a spurt of blood, as if the leg itself had rejected it. He borrowed some of Hampton's whiskey and poured it on the wound, and that hurt, too. Then he loosened the tourniquet and tied the dirty bandana around the leg as a bandage. When the bleeding stopped, he would expose the wound to the open air.

He fell back against the dirt with his eyes closed. Sweat was pouring down his face. Something scratched his good leg. He looked down. It was the dog Sparky, grinning. The terrier pawed Jake's leg again, insistent. Jake laughed. What a crazy world it was. He reached out and scratched the dog's ears.

The day stretched on, seemingly without end. Jake grew dizzy with heat and pain. He slipped in and out of reality. He heard an occasional rifle shot, heard an occasional bullet zip overhead. He heard the wounded horse crying, and he wished it would stop.

At one point in the afternoon, Blade jumped on the lip of the water hole, waving his revolver and screaming at the invisible enemy, "Come on, you bastards! Come on! Come out and fight! What's the matter with you?" Shots rang out. Hampton and Harvey Reed grabbed the overseer and wrestled him to safety.

When night came, it was like an afterthought. No one cared any longer. The emigrants savored the relief from the sun, but they knew that it was the last thing they would savor in this world. One way or another, from hunger or heat or Indians, this time tomorrow they would all be dead.

24

Another dream-haunted night passed. Another blisteringly hot day began. The Indians did not fire at the water hole anymore. They didn't have to. The sun, the lack of food, and the muddy water were doing their job for them. The Indians were still there, though. Periodic clouds of dust on the horizon told of horses coming and going.

The smell of decomposing men and horses grew stronger and stronger. The emigrants choked on it. They could not get away from it. Frank Sloane's body was visible in the mesquite. Something had been eating it. The wounded horse had mercifully ceased its agonized whinnying.

Jake's leg throbbed with the rhythmic insistence of a drumbeat. His head was swimming with fever. Despite the heat, he wrapped himself in his blanket to ward off the chills that came over him. He bit back groans of pain so hard that his lip bled. Dan Essex, with a wound much worse, wasn't complaining; so Jake couldn't complain either.

The rest of the emigrants lay weakly in the sun and waited for the inevitable. Food was running low, but they didn't feel like eating. They were too tired to dig for water. The dog was stretched out in the meager shade provided by Jake's body. Jake didn't know whether the animal was alive or not. Harvey Reed pulled from the rags of his shirt the red-white-and-green "EXCELSIOR" flag that had once adorned the New York Gold Hunters' Conestoga. He stared at it numbly. He was a long way from the accounting office on Wall Street where he had first conceived the idea of going to California.

Late in the morning, Ethan's bandage was removed. There was no point in keeping it on. The boy was going to die, either way. He trembled while Mrs. Skeffington unwrapped it. Cautiously he opened his eyes, then his face melted with relief as he blinked against the strong sunlight. "I can see," he said. "Thank God. You was right, Jake."

"How good are they?" Jake asked. He was surprised at such a quick recovery. He was surprised that Ethan had recovered at all.

"They ain't what they used to be," Ethan admitted. "Not yet. But they're good enough I can take my place again." He gathered his weapons and moved off slowly, getting used to his renewed vision. Alone of the emigrants, he had found a reason to be happy for the little time that was left to him.

Essex watched Ethan go. "I'd like to be moved near Jake and Woody," he told Mrs. Skeffington. "There's nothing more you can do for me, anyway; we both know that. I'd rather finish up with them."

Jake and Woodhouse carried the ex-sailor up the side of the water hole, where they laid him down gently. Mrs. Skeffington followed, with a rifle and pistols, prepared to assume a position on the line. Jake had a hard time standing upright. He was shivering with fever as he addressed the colonel's wife. "I'd like to thank you for all your efforts, ma'am." It sounded like he was saying goodbye to her. Probably he was.

"Nonsense," the old woman said. "I was only doing my part." Ragged, filthy, and armed to the teeth, she still managed to look dignified.

"Still, it can't have been easy," Jake said. "This ain't what you're used to."

"Young man, I've spent most of my life living in tents, under the eyes of hundred of private soldiers. Don't you worry about me."

They were distracted by shouting from across the water hole. "I can't stand it! I can't stand any more!" It was Blade again. He was delirious. He stumbled for the top of the water hole, but Hampton rose and knocked him down. The blow seemed to bring the muscular overseer to his senses. He sat up, rubbing his jaw.

Hampton turned. He was gaunt now. His swollen left eye was opening a bit, even as the other eye grew puffy from the sun. "Blade's got a point, Jake. Why don't we just end it? Instead of dying here like rats, why don't we go out there and take as many of the red bastards as we can with us? Anything's better than this."

Jake pulled himself together. He grinned with what he hoped looked like confidence. "We'll hold out here. There's still a chance they'll pull out. I don't believe in giving up."

"You must believe in miracles, then," Hampton said.

"I seen stranger things happen," Jake replied. He hadn't, but it sounded good. He wondered if Hampton's idea was right. He wondered if he didn't want to force an end himself because he was scared to go out and face death like a man.

The company accepted Jake's decision. They settled in to wait.

Jake lay back against the earth and stared at the brassy sky. He lost all sensation of time. The sun was a molten ball of fire overhead. The heat was stultifying. It was sucking the life from him. He couldn't move. The end was near.

Yellow Wolf has won, Jake thought. All he has to do is wait a bit longer. He won't have to lift a finger. Jake granted the old chief his victory. Yellow Wolf was the better man.

Beside Jake, Essex's breath grew more and more shallow. Because he had a stomach wound, the ex-Navy man could not be given water. Men with stomach wounds did not live, but it didn't matter, because none of them would live through this. Essex laughed weakly. When he spoke, his voice was thin and dry, like the rustling of old leaves. "This isn't the end I expected. I always thought I'd die of old age, loaded down with honors and surrounded by adoring grandchildren."

"Always fancied I'd be done in by a jealous husband, meself," muttered Woodhouse from Jake's other side.

Essex's voice grew weaker. He turned his emerald green eyes on Jake and smiled. He was as calm as ever, but there was a harsh rattle in his throat. "We gave it a good try, didn't we, Jake? Too bad we didn't win. You did a fine job. It's been a pleasure . . . serving with you . . . Captain."

Jake turned away. He hadn't done a fine job. He was a fraud, an impostor. He couldn't let this end without his friend knowing the truth about him. He had to clear his conscience. He stared at his scarred hands. "Dan, I . . . I got to tell you something. About me. About Chapultapec, and all that. Dan, I never . . ." He looked over. Essex's lips were parted. His eyes stared sightlessly into space.

Jake closed his own eyes tightly and turned away. Tears ran down his cheeks.

"What is it?" Woodhouse said. "Oh, Christ, is Dan . . . ?"

Behind them was a noise of scuffling feet. "Look out!" shouted Mrs. Skeffington.

Jake raised himself to see copper-colored bodies leaping into the water hole. He had an impression of paint and beads and breechclouts. There must have been a dozen of them. As he floundered for one of his Navy Colts, he saw Woodhouse rise. A brave with his face painted yellow shot the Englishman in the chest with an old Paterson Colt. Woodhouse staggered off balance and fell, even as Mrs. Skeffington shot the brave who had downed him.

Jake had no more time to look. A squat brave was sliding down the bank toward him. Jake shot him in the chest. A feathered Kiowa came at him with his war ax raised.

Jake somehow ducked the blow. He shot at the Indian, but his revolver misfired. Cursing, Jake stepped forward and slammed the revolver into the Indian's head with such force that the barrel flew off. The Indian groaned and dropped to the ground.

The water hole was a confused swirl of hand-to-hand fighting, of yells and shots. The dog was barking. Across the water hole, a powerful-looking Indian was pulling his ax from Blade's skull. Jake saw a shaven patch in the Indian's hair; he saw black stripes across his face. It was Yellow Wolf. Yellow Wolf stood and yelled, *"Aah-hey!"* He was claiming coup and shouting for witnesses.

Jake threw away the useless pistol butt. With a renewed strength born of desperation, he lumbered after Yellow Wolf with his bowie knife. He wondered irrationally why he hadn't drawn another revolver, but it was too late to change.

Yellow Wolf sensed him coming. He turned, and Jake threw himself upon him. Jake tried to stab the Indian with the knife, but Yellow Wolf grabbed Jake's wrist and deflected the knife down and away so that the blade only slashed his side. At the same time, Yellow Wolf flailed at Jake with his ax, and Jake grabbed the Indian's arm in turn.

Jake had the advantage of surprise and momentum, and at first he drove Yellow Wolf backward. But the Indian's superior strength began to tell. They grappled, struggling for advantage, then Yellow Wolf hooked Jake's leg and bore him onto his back. They rolled around, each holding the other's wrist, grunting, hitting. The Indian's chest pressed on Jake's face. Jake tasted blood and sour sweat. He smelled the buffalo dung with which the Indian greased his hair. Jake tried to push Yellow Wolf off, while Yellow Wolf tried to swing his ax. Jake caught a knee in the eye. He saw stars and cried out, but he hung on. He tried to throw his elbows, but he couldn't get leverage. Yellow Wolf had Jake's knife hand in a viselike grip, while he tried to work his own hand free for a blow. Jake kicked his legs, trying to throw the Indian off. Suddenly Yellow Wolf bit a chunk out of Jake's nose. Jake yelled in shock, and Yellow Wolf wrenched his ax hand free. He swung the weapon. Jake moved, and the blade hit his shoulder. There was a searing pain, then Jake had the Indian's arm again. The two men squirmed around. Jake couldn't hold Yellow Wolf's wrist much longer; his wounded arm was on fire. His back was being ground into the dirt. Yellow Wolf strained, baring his worn brown teeth. Jake smelled his horrible breath. Yellow Wolf wrenched his ax hand free again. He sat on Jake's chest and lifted the ax for a killing blow. Jake raised his arm weakly to block it. The two men's eyes met. Again that curious look came into the old chief's face, as if he recognized someone, as if Jake reminded him of someone. There was a moment of hesitation, and Jake felt the Indian's grip on his knife arm weaken. Desperately, Jake yanked his knife hand free and jabbed the eighteen-inch blade up under the chief's ribs. Yellow Wolf cried out. Jake pulled out the blade. He thrust it upward again, twisting it deep into the chief's chest. Again the Indian cried out, and his cry was full of pain. Blood squirted down on Jake. Yellow Wolf looked into Jake's eyes with a last flash of recognition; of acknowledgment; and Jake suddenly wished that he hadn't stabbed him. He felt that strange bond between them again. The old chief was trembling now. He dropped his war ax. He reached out and touched Jake's cheek, gently. Then he toppled forward. His head was alongside Jake's; his sightless eyes were still locked on those of the white man. Jake had to force himself to break their gaze.

Jake lay back, sad, hating himself. He rolled Yellow Wolf's body away. He'd forgotten the battle around him. The last surviving Indians were disappearing over the rim of the water hole. Harvey Reed was firing his pistols after them. With their chief dead, they had lost heart and run.

Jake looked around. Ethan was on the ground; blood flowed from wounds in his neck and shoulder. Mrs. Skeffington leaned against the bank of earth, breathing heavily, two dead braves at her feet. Hampton was standing, holding his wounded side, watching Jake with an expression that Jake could not read. Jake counted seven Indian bodies.

Incredibly, Woodhouse was sitting up, his revolver smoking. The Englishman shook the cobwebs from his head. He reached into his coat and pulled out his watch. The watch case was shattered; it must have stopped the yellow-faced Indian's bullet. Woodhouse opened it. The watch tinkled the first notes of "Rule Britannia," then it plunked a horribly off-key note and died. "Mother won't like this," Woodhouse said.

"Oh, my merciful God, look!" Harvey was yelling from the lip of the water hole, pointing wildly. "They're leaving! All of them! They're leaving!"

Jake stood awkwardly, painfully. Blood ran from his hacked shoulder. Yellow Wolf's blood soaked his clothes. His leg throbbed worse than ever. He limped up the side of the water hole, beside Harvey, and looked out. A huge dust cloud showed where many horses were retreating to the northwest.

"Why?" Jake said.

Yellow Wolf must have been desperate to avenge his son. He must have talked a small group of braves into creeping close to the water hole and following him to glory or death. But why? The old chief had the emigrants dead; all he had to do was wait a few hours. Why had he thrown away his victory? And why were the rest of the Indians leaving now?

Jake climbed out of the water hole. He searched the horizon, then he stopped as he saw the reason for the Indians' departure. Away to the south was another cloud of dust, approaching them. The cloud was long and narrow, made by riders in regular or semi-regular formation.

"White men coming," Jake croaked. He was so happy that he could hardly say the words. "We're saved. It's over."

The minute this is over . . .

The emigrants reacted first with stunned surprise, then with joy. Those who were not hurt rushed up to look. They were laughing, crying, praying, giving thanks on their knees. Amid the jubilation, Jake felt a sudden chill. His hair prickled, and some sixth sense warned him that he was in greater danger than ever before.

The minute this is over, I'm going to kill you.

That same sixth sense had him reaching behind his back for the Dragoon .44. It had him turning and stepping sideways at the same moment as a bullet whispered past his cheek. He saw Tyler Hampton staggering across the water hole toward him, holding his bloody side, smoke coming from his pistol, face black with hate.

Everything seemed to happen in slow motion. Someone else—not Jake—seemed to raise the .44. Someone else seemed to cock it and squeeze the trigger—once for himself, twice for Dan Essex, a third time for old Yellow Wolf. Someone else seemed to be crying out in rage and grief as the heavy slugs plowed into Hampton's chest and blasted him across the water hole onto his back, dead.

There was silence. Everyone was looking at Jake. Powder smoke drifted around him, into his eyes, into his nostrils. He stared down at Hampton's torn and bloody corpse. The comradeship, the offer of a drink, it had all been a trick. Hampton had been trying to set Jake up. He had intended to kill Jake all along. He had played Jake for a fool, when all that Jake had wanted was a friend.

Jake turned away—away from Hampton, away from the emigrants. He looked at the .44. Then, with a sob of anguish, he took the pistol and heaved it as far as he could.

25

When the ex-slave Culpepper led a company of Texas Militia to the water hole at Comanche Crossing, they found Jake sitting by himself in the afternoon heat, reading Woodhouse's copy of *David Copperfield*.

The militia company was not large. The Comanches might have been able to handle them, had they gone about it right. Most of the militiamen were in their late teens or early twenties, dressed in flannel shirts or buckskins, hung all over with rifles and shotguns and revolvers. Their leader was a few years older, with a roundish, jolly face. Long, curly hair stuck out from under his hat, and he sported the obligatory drooping mustache. He wore no badge or insignia of rank, nor did any of his men. They looked about them, at the bodies and the litter and the tattered survivors. They wrinkled their noses at the stench of death.

Jake turned back to *David Copperfield*, while the rest of the emigrants greeted their rescuers. "Culpepper!" shouted Harvey Reed, pumping the black man's hand. "We thought you were dead!"

Under his glazed hat, the normally impassive Culpepper laughed. He shook Woodhouse's hand; he shook Mrs. Skeffington's hand. He was not used to being a hero. "Hell, I thought I was dead, myself. Damn near I *was* dead. When them Injuns come yellin' out of the dark, I don't know who was scaredest, that horse or me. It was purely luck we got away."

Culpepper dismounted, stiffly because of his bad leg,

and led the militia commander to where Jake was sitting. Jake carefully marked his place in the book and looked up.

To the militiaman, Culpepper said, "This is Jake Moran, our captain. Jake, this is Captain J. W. Venable of the Texas Militia."

Jake rose. He moved slowly, deliberately, so that he wouldn't fall. His fevered eyes drifted in and out of focus. Each throb of his leg was agony, and his wounded shoulder felt like it was going to fall off. He shook hands with the militiaman, and that made his sore hand hurt, too. "Glad to see you, Captain. Glad to see you, too, Culpepper. Real glad."

"Glad to be here," Culpepper said. "I run into this patrol about a half a day out of Fort Davis. Course I had a little problem persuadin' them I was really free. Hadn't been for that paper of yours, I'd be decoratin' some tree 'long about now."

"Reckon you surprised some of these folks, comin' back like you did, 'stead of lightin' out for Mexico," Jake said.

The black man grinned. "Reckon I surprised myself."

The round-faced Venable looked at Jake with undisguised admiration. He had the appearance of an educated man, and Jake guessed he was a lawyer. From the state capital at Austin, probably, or from Houston or San Antone. Trying to build a military record for a run at politics. "Captain Moran, I must say you're about the coolest customer I've ever run across. After all you've been through, how you can sit here reading a book beats me hollow."

There were mutters of agreement from the militiamen—from the emigrants, as well.

Jake didn't say anything. These people didn't realize that he was doing the only thing he could to keep from screaming, to keep from going completely mad. If he let his emotions run away with him, he would never be able to rein them in again.

Captain Venable's admiration for Jake increased as the other emigrants told him about the company's march from

San Antonio and the siege at the water hole. No one mentioned how Tyler Hampton had died. They let him be remembered as a valiant Indian fighter.

"Yellow Wolf!" Venable said, as the story reached its climax. "He's dead? Where?"

Harvey Reed showed him the body. Venable whistled low. "I never saw him up close before. By Christmas, killing this old devil was quite a feat, Captain Moran. Quite a feat. It takes a load off us, I can tell you. Yellow Wolf's been a scourge to Texas for twenty-five years, him and his son both. You've done us a real service."

Jake remained silent. He had not killed Yellow Wolf. Yellow Wolf had let him do it. He could still feel the old chief's touch on his cheek.

There was a pistol shot as someone put down the wounded horse. There were more shots as some wounded Comanches were similarly dispatched. Venable went on, sweat running down his ample cheeks, "Captain Moran, yours is an amazing story. Truly it is. You have established a record of bravery and endurance with this company that any man could envy—and believe me, sir, I do envy it. I want to express the gratitude of the entire state of Texas. There's not much I can do for you in a material sense, unfortunately, but I can commission you an honorary captain in our militia."

"Thank you," Jake said. His voice seemed to come from far away.

"Wait, there *is* one thing I can give." Venable took off his revolver belt and removed its Lone Star buckle. He handed the buckle to Jake. "Please, take this as a symbol of your commission, and of our thanks."

Jake looked at the big, handsomely polished brass buckle.

"Heavy, isn't it?" Venable said. "Heavy enough to stop a bullet. Who knows, maybe one day it will save your life." He laughed.

"Maybe," Jake said. Venable acted like Jake must enjoy the fighting, the killing.

One of the militiamen was a self-styled horse doctor. He cleaned out Ethan's and Jake's wounds, sewed them up, and tended the minor injuries of the other emigrants. Ethan had lost a quantity of blood, but he would be all right.

While the "doctor" worked, the other militiamen buried the white dead. The Indian bodies were dragged far from the water hole and left to rot, after they had been scalped and their weapons and accoutrements had been taken as souvenirs. One youngster was just raising Yellow Wolf's hair for the knife when Jake hobbled forward and snarled, "No."

The boy looked up, grinning. "Want it for yourself, huh?"

"I want it left on," Jake said. He gazed fiercely at the boy. His chest was rising and falling rapidly. He knew the spectacle he must have presented—wide-eyed, bloody, emaciated. "Let the old man enter his afterlife. He deserves that much."

The boy glanced nervously over at Venable, then he let down Yellow Wolf's hair. "All . . . all right. Sure. If that's what you want."

"Rider comin', Cap'n," cried another militiaman.

Venable turned. He squinted into the sun's hot glare. "We sent scouts after the Indians," he told Jake. "This is one of 'em coming back."

The rider reined in and dismounted. He was another boy, wiry and blue-eyed, with a straggly attempt at a blond mustache.

"Report," Venable said.

"Them Comanch' is headed for the Staked Plains, Cap'n, just like you said. And they're leavin' a trail of dead behind 'em you wouldn't believe."

"Men wounded by Captain Moran and his company?"

"No, Cap'n. This is different. These are sick. Lieutenant Pettigrew, he says it looks like they died of the cholera."

Jake straightened. Icy fingers seemed to wrap themselves around his spine. Cholera. So that was why Yellow Wolf had attacked. His warriors had somehow contracted cholera from the company's leavings—from the bodies they had dug up, or the infected clothing, or the wagons. While the emigrants had been besieged here at the water hole, the Comanches had not been relaxing. They had been dying. Terrified, the majority of the Indians had finally fled for home, while Yellow Wolf and a few others had made a last attempt at killing the white enemies who had brought this horror upon them. Yellow Wolf may have feared that he had the disease himself. He may have decided that he had nothing to lose, that in a day or two he would be dead anyway. Now his tribesmen were running to their fastnesses in the Llano Estacado, not realizing that they could not outrun cholera, not aware that they carried the disease with them. Jake could picture only too well how the cholera would sweep through the Comanche villages, killing with an efficiency the white men's guns could never match, reducing the Indian population by a degree that could not be made up, destroying a people.

Venable was talking. "If this is true, it's wonderful news, Captain. Wonderful. That was a brilliant idea of yours, to plant your infected goods where the savages would find them. You may have done us an even bigger service than we first imagined. Every buck that dies of cholera is one less to murder innocent settlers down here in Texas. Every dead squaw is one less to breed warriors. Every dead child is one less we have to kill when he grows up. You and your company have helped make the frontier safer for a generation, perhaps for all time. Texas will bless your memory."

Jake turned away. He felt sick.

When the buried emigrants had been prayed over, Venable addressed the six remaining members of Hampton's California Company. "Gentlemen—and madam—I give you your choice. My men and I can escort you back to San Antonio, or we can take you to Fort Davis and then to El Paso, from where you may continue your journey to California. We are at your disposal in the matter. The decision is yours.''

Jake didn't have to think about it. He wanted to go back to San Antonio. The city should be safe by now; the cholera should have run its course. From San Antonio he would get to New Orleans and take ship for California. He would sign on as an ordinary seaman if he had to.

He looked at his little command, his first command. An Englishman who painted pictures of birds, an aging Army wife, a crippled black man, a half-blind farm boy, a skinny clerk, and a dog that barked all night. ''What do you want to do?'' he asked them.

Woodhouse raised an eyebrow and grinned. ''Tell the man, Jake.''

''You're our leader,'' Mrs. Skeffington said.

''We'll do what you say,'' Culpepper said.

''That's right.'' Harvey Reed nodded.

''It sure is,'' Ethan said from his litter.

Jake could read the looks on their faces. He knew the answer they wanted. He knew the answer they expected from the Hero of Chapultapec.

''What do you say?'' Venable asked. ''Do you wish to turn back?''

Jake drew himself up. ''Turn back, hell. We're going to California.''

ABOUT THE AUTHOR

Robert W. Broomall has been a journalist, draftee, bartender, and civil servant. His main interests are travel and history, especially that of the Old West and the Middle Ages. In addition to DEAD MAN'S CROSSING, he is the author of THE BANK ROBBER and DEAD MAN'S CANYON, the first book in the Jake Moran western series. He is currently at work on a new book featuring Jake Moran. Mr. Broomall lives in Maryland, with his wife and children.

FAWCETT ROUNDS UP THE *Best of the West*